They shed their clothes and quietly bury them beneath leaves and needles. The night air is cold and Paulie feels goose bumps rising. *This is nothing*, he thinks, *compared to what it's about to be.*

"Suspense, heartbreak, a healthy dose of athletics— this novel has everything that Crutcher's longtime fans have come to expect, and more."—*Kirkus Reviews*

"Some books get you in their talons and won't let go. It's got all the chewy goodness of a Crutcher teen athlete novel, ramped up with a mystery that unfolds in a most creepy way."—Elizabeth Bluemle, *PW Shelftalker*

"This is vintage Crutcher, with authentic dialogue, a school setting, lots of sports, and sympathetic characters that feel as if they had walked out of another Crutcher novel. This time, the suspense and action are ratcheted way up, though, and the result is a nailbiter with well-planted hints that lead up to a surprising, satisfying resolution."—*Booklist*

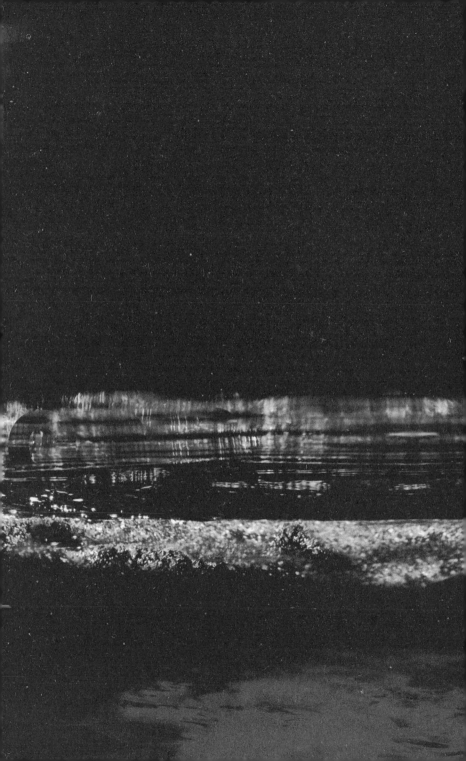

CHRIS CRUTCHER

PERIOD 8

 Greenwillow Books, An Imprint of HarperCollins*Publishers*

Period 8
Copyright © 2013 by Chris Crutcher
First published in hardcover in 2013 by Greenwillow Books; first paperback publication, 2014.
All rights reserved. No part of this book may be used or reproduced in any manner whatsoever without written permission except in the case of brief quotations embodied in critical articles and reviews. Printed in the United States of America. For information address HarperCollins Children's Books, a division of HarperCollins Publishers, 195 Broadway, New York, NY 10007.
www.epicreads.com
The text of this book is set in Baskerville MT.
Book design by Sylvie Le Floc'h
Interior artwork copyright © by S. Pytel/Shutterstock.com

Library of Congress Cataloging-in-Publication Data
Crutcher, Chris.
Period 8 / Chris Crutcher.
pages cm.
"Greenwillow Books."
Summary: Period 8 has always been a safe haven and high school senior Paulie "The Bomb" Baum a constant attendee, but as Paulie, Hannah, their friends, and a sympathetic teacher try to unravel the mystery of a missing classmate, the ultimate bully takes aim at the school.
ISBN 978-0-06-191480-5 (hardback)—ISBN 978-0-06-191481-2 (library ed.)—
ISBN 978-0-06-191482-9 (pbk ed.)
[1. Clubs—Fiction. 2. Missing children—Fiction.
3. Bullies—Fiction. Kidnapping—Fiction.
5. Sexual abuse—Fiction. 6. High schools—Fiction. 7. Schools—Fiction. 8. Mystery and detective stories.] I. Title. II. Title: Period eight.
PZ7.C89Per 2013 [Fic]—dc23 2012046726
17 PC/RRDC 10 9 8 7 6 5 4 3
First Edition

 Greenwillow Books

For Liz,
in memory of Tony

PERIOD 8

A teenage girl steps out of the bathroom, clutching her blouse tight at the collar where the buttons are missing, walks across the grimy carpet, and slips her feet into her flip-flops. The man sits on the end of the bed pulling on his shoes, snaps the clasp on his watchband, pushes back his thinning hair. The girl stands, staring at him.

The man doesn't speak.

"Uh," she says in a whisper. "Can you help me get back to my car?"

"Sorry, darlin'," he says. "By the way, what's your name? Who do I ask for?"

"I'm Star," she says.

He smiles. "Star. Where's your young friend, Star?"

She shrugs.

"I'd like to help," he says, glancing around the room, "but I've, uh, gotta run." He picks his sport jacket off the floor, shakes it, puts it on. With his hand on the door knob he turns. "That was nice," he says. "I'm, uh, sure someone will take you to your car."

The door closes behind him and the girl drops to her knees, face in hands, gasping for breath. When she's under control she grabs her purse and steps outside, squinting into the sun high in the sky. A familiar car pulls to a stop in the street and she hurries to get in.

Near midnight Paulie Bomb pulls his VW Beetle onto the shoulder of Ridgeview Drive and kills the engine. He's just finished his shift at The Rocket Bakery and Coffee House, where Hannah kept him company for the last hour. He releases the seat back a couple of inches and breathes deep, staring over the blanket of city lights below.

"You're bringing me here to *park?*" Hannah says, laughing. "This is a *Beetle.* I'm used to better accommodations."

"I need . . ."

"What?"

". . . to talk."

"Right here," she says, leaning over to kiss him. "World's best listener."

The kiss is long and hot and causes him to hesitate. "I gotta be sure we're goin' farther."

Hannah smiles, slides her hand up his thigh. "Why wouldn't we? Everything—"

"I cheated." He closes his eyes tight.

Her hand comes off his leg. "You'd better be talking about the chem test."

"I wish I was. Let me explain . . ."

Hannah presses her back against the passenger door. "Did you put your dick in someone who wasn't me?"

"Hannah, Jesus, yes. But—"

"Then there's nothing to say. Take me home."

"Will you just—"

"Don't say another word. Start the car and take me home, in *fucking silence*, or I'm walking."

Paulie starts to say something but Hannah reaches behind her for the door handle. He starts the car. So much for the world's best listener.

Paulie crests the knoll on the old highway leading to the landing dock on the city side of Diamond Lake. He cuts the engine and coasts to a stop, then sits, staring at the perfect upside-down early morning twin of Smalley's Peak in the glass-still water. It's late March—still cool in the Pacific Northwest—first outdoor workout of the year; the water will be *cold*, probably mid-fifties. If he doesn't lose feeling in his fingers and toes, he'll coax Logs out here this afternoon. Bruce Logsdon teaches science and social studies at Heller High, runs Period 8 at lunchtime, and swims open water with Paulie Bomb—Paul Baum. Logs requires Paulie to test the water temperature early each spring before immersing his own body.

Paulie pops the trunk lock and hauls out his triathlete's wetsuit. At least his nuts will be warm. Like *that* will ever matter again. Oh, Hannah.

He hits the water, involuntarily sucking air as the cold leaks in. *The colder the better.* He deserves this. Even so, he pees in self-defense, his only means to counter the ice-watery fingers creeping around his ribcage and into his crotch. He swims away from shore for about a hundred yards as his body heat warms the water inside the suit. He turns parallel to the shore and strokes, finding a cadence he can hold over the next two hours. He knows how to play games to allay the monotony; fifty strokes hard, fifty strokes easy; a hundred strokes hard, fifty easy; a hundred-fifty hard, fifty easy, and on and on. An hour up and an hour back. He has taught himself to breathe on either side in order to keep the shore in sight and swim a relatively straight line. On this morning, working on zero sleep, he holds an even pace; no intervals. Just his sweet, sweet Hannah wedged in his frontal lobe. His *gone* Hannah.

Paulie Bomb could have any girl at Heller High, according to most of his buddies. He's tall and built like an athletic *machine*. None of his features are classic, but his slightly crooked nose, shaggy brown hair, and dark watery eyes fetch him more between-class approaches than his friends can stand. He hears, "She wants to have your babies," in his ear at least twice daily. Most often from Justin Chenier.

But then came Hannah.

Paulie raps lightly on the door to room 137, Homestead Studio Suites, an extended-stay hotel less than a mile from his house.

The door opens on a man in his early forties dressed in khakis, an open collared blue gingham shirt, and Birkenstocks. "Hey, Dad," Paulie says. "We still on for breakfast?"

"Indeed we are," Roger Baum says. "How much time you got?"

"Much as we want," Paulie says. "My first two periods are free this morning."

"I should have gone to your high school," his dad says. "Let me get my jacket and in five minutes we'll be knee-deep in pancakes."

"How long before you're back home?" Paulie asks as they slide into a booth at the IHOP across the street.

"Shouldn't be long," his father says. "Your mother and I have been talking. We had dinner last night."

"She seems pretty determined this time."

"You must have talked to her before we had dinner," his father says. "She's coming around."

The waitress brings the "bottomless" pot of coffee and takes their orders: a sausage and cheese omelet with hash browns, wheat toast, and juice for Paulie, pigs-in-a-blanket for his dad.

"Man, Dad, don't you get tired of it?" Paulie asks, as she leaves to put in the order.

Roger Baum closes his eyes, shakes his head slowly. "I do get tired. Things just . . . you know way too much. You shouldn't be dealing with this."

"Right," Paulie says, "but I do, like, every time."

"Your mom should keep this between me and her."

"Come on, Dad, what's she supposed to say when you're home one night and packing your stuff the next? It's not like she complains to me. When things are shitty it's obvious."

"I guess," his dad says. "I just don't like you having to deal with it."

Only way that's going to happen is if you stop doing it. Paulie sits back. This conversation ends the same every time. "I have personal reasons for asking, Dad. Why do you do it?"

His dad sighs. "I don't need the judgment, Paulie. I'll talk, but you don't bring the guilt."

If you're feeling guilty, it's not 'cause I'm bringing it. "Fair enough."

They spare the waitress as she places their breakfasts in front of them.

"Part of it is the job," his father says when she walks away. "The stress of it, the *high,* and then the boredom. The call comes and you're in the truck, lights flashing and siren wailing, weaving in and out of traffic, then you're scrambling to save somebody's life or get them to emergency where somebody else can. You do all you can and then *bam!* It's over. You either did it or not.

"Then you go for a couple of beers, which turns into a half rack, feeling like a hero, or at least a near-hero." He looks away. "Sometimes inventing glory that never was, and if your partner is female, things get . . . well. You get to thinking you're the only ones who understand. Next thing you know . . ."

Paulie says, "Wait."

"You promised not to judge."

Paulie throws up his hands. "No judgment, but that was *this* time. Time before it was that lady at the fitness place and unless I missed the newsflash, *it* wasn't on fire. . . ."

Paulie's dad leans forward, elbows on the table. "You're right. Bullshit excuse. It's . . . *character* for lack of a better word. Sometimes it feels like it's in my DNA."

"This is the part I want to know."

"I was twenty-three when your mother and I got married," Paulie's dad says. "You know the story. There's nothing I wouldn't have done to get your mother interested. We broke up for a short while when we were seniors and I swore if I ever got her back, I'd never chance losing her again."

"Why'd you break up that first time?" Paulie asks.

His dad's eyes close.

"That's what I thought. How'd it happen?"

"I was the cool jock and this girl your mom *hated*—her name was Charlotte Weaver—was moving in on me. Your mom was out of town and Charlotte stopped over to see if I wanted to do something."

"And the something was her," Paulie said.

"The something was her. I felt bad afterward—scared—but I thought I got away with it. I mean, back of a car, no witnesses."

"You tell on yourself?" Paulie asks. DNA couldn't be *that* strong.

His dad frowns. "Hell no, I didn't tell on myself. Charlotte went public. Sneaky. Told one of her friends she knew couldn't keep her mouth shut. That was the whole point of snagging me. I was just a dumb jock who didn't see it coming. Sex gives girls power sometimes. You have to watch out for that."

"Sex gives boys power sometimes too, Dad." Paulie takes a big bite of his omelet. "So after that Mom didn't see the writing on the wall? How'd you guys get back together?"

"Man, I begged. I crawled. It was the last time it would

ever happen. If she'd give me *one more chance* I'd make it up to her. Now I knew what I had to lose."

"How'd *that* go?"

"Pretty well, actually. We were married ten years before it happened again."

"Then the stress and boredom?" A hint of sarcasm. "Okay, okay, no judgment."

Paulie's dad pours them each a refill. "Naw, Paulie, you're right, stress and boredom *is* bullshit. Like I said, I was twenty-three and I made a promise in front of a preacher and your grandparents and a whole bunch of our friends that I had no idea I couldn't keep. In my defense, I shouldn't have had to make that promise; nobody should. Nobody tells you when you're your age that you'll likely be a different guy when you're thirty and a different guy from that when you're forty-five. I'm not just talking about sex. I'm talking worldview. I'm talking experience."

"One thing I wish," Paulie says.

"What's that?"

"That next time you'll just go."

"And stay gone?"

"There wouldn't be any 'child of divorce' BS or anything close. I love both you guys. But I hate you when you come back and I hate her for letting you back, just because I don't want to relive it the next time. Maybe it's selfish, but you guys just end up looking weak, and I gotta tell you, I'd a lot rather have divorced parents than weak parents."

"I didn't know you felt that way."

"'Cause I've been too chicken to tell you," Paulie says. "Did you know last year when I was running for student body president, Arney used your and Mom's relationship against me?"

"What?"

"Yeah. You know, could people trust me. All that bullshit about how far the apple falls from the tree."

"That son of a bitch," his dad says. "Why didn't you kick his ass?"

"I mentioned that possibility to him. He claimed one of his 'strategists' made the signs without telling him."

"God, Paulie, I'm sorry . . ."

"Actually," Paulie says, "it's about the only time it worked in my favor. Last thing in the world I needed was to be student body president. I was just showing off."

"I never liked that kid. He's such a—"

"He's just Arney," Paulie says. "Wants to grow up to be a politician. He was doing what the big boys do. C'mon, let's get out of here. Gotta at least make an appearance at school."

His father grabs the tab. "You do know," he says, "that you look like shit."

"What are you doing here?" Logs stands in his classroom doorway and pinches the back of Paulie's neck.

"Bathroom break."

"Does my classroom look like the can?"

Paulie frowns and smiles. "Don't make it so *easy*, man."

Logs glances at his watch. "Ten minutes to Period 8. What class are you scamming?"

"Calc."

"Unless you drop your pants and squat, or otherwise prove you think my classroom is the crapper, you're gonna get me in trouble standing here in the hall."

"No trouble," Paulie says. "Jus and I know that stuff better than Mr. Ridge. When I asked to go to the can I thought he was going to send Justin with me." He nods toward the door. "We can go in if it makes you feel better."

Logs laughs. "You're right," he says, "no trouble. My last year. They threaten to fire me, I take the rest of it in sick time. I've got more than three years' worth stacked up."

Paulie stares down the deserted hall. "Man, why aren't you taking it?"

"And miss the opportunity to harass you and your posse right up to the last day? I think not." Logs motions him inside the classroom. "Hey, you don't know anything about Mary Wells, do you? She hasn't been in P-8 for nearly a week."

Paulie looks out the window, focuses on a tree squirrel. "She hasn't been in government either," he says.

"Perfect attendance for four years," Logs says. "It's unusual. I'll check with the office." He straightens papers on his desk. "So, how was the water this morning? How long 'til it's warm enough for my wrinkled butt?"

Paulie smiles. "It came seepin' into my suit, my testes headed for my heart. I don't expect them back until maybe the Fourth."

"I remember the days when I could tolerate that." Logs laughs. "Back when I needed 'em anyway."

"You are dangerously close to TMI," Paulie says, and hesitates. "Actually, I might be in that boat myself, for a different reason." He shakes his head slowly, hoisting himself onto a desktop. "Man, Mr. Logs, I messed up big time."

Logs watches Paulie's eyes cloud over. "Spill it, young 'un. The doctor is in."

■ ■ ■

"How'd she find out?" Logs asks after hearing Paulie's story.

"I told her."

"Did the girl—and I appreciate your not revealing her identity, speaking of Too Much Information—did she threaten to tell?"

"God no," Paulie says. "She begged *me* not to."

"Did somebody catch you?"

"*No.*"

"Then why . . . how can I put this? It's not exactly standard operating procedure for a young buck such as yourself to cheat, get away clean, then rat yourself out. I mean, don't get me wrong . . . Jesus, I'm glad this is my last year."

"You think I should have kept quiet?"

"Advice of this particular nature is way above my pay grade," Logs says. "I'm just saying that in my experience working with kids . . . hell, in my experience *being* a kid . . . well, like I started to say, a jury of your peers might deem you short on survival skills."

"*That's* who I want passing judgment on me," Paulie says back. "My peers."

"I'm just saying. . . ."

"I know. Tell me something, Mr. Logs—if I had come to you before I told her, what woulda been your advice?"

Logs leans back in his chair, hands knitted behind his head. "I would have done any and everything in my power not to give it."

"How come?"

Logs shrugs. "To avoid hypocrisy, I guess."

Paulie frowns.

"You know, buddy, there's this unspoken teacher's code thing where I'm supposed to give you 'moral' advice." He glances at his watch. "But it's too close to P-8 and too close to my retirement for that. Look, I don't know the circumstances under which you committed this heinous act, and I'll thank you to keep it that way, but I'm rushing headlong into the age of mandatory Medicare. I went on my first date at age nine, took Amy Velar to the Shrine Circus. I knew more about male-female interaction *then*."

"You're gonna have to do better than that if you want to be my guru," Paulie says.

"If I were your guru, I'd have to share responsibility for the crazy shit you do. I have enough crazy shit of my own, thank you."

Paulie runs his hands through his hair, his gaze drifting to the ceiling.

"Kidding aside," Logs says. "There's not a good reason to lie to people we care about. And we should honor our commitments. In a perfect world, right? I'm assuming you and Hannah were exclusive."

Paulie nods.

"So if you had come to me beforehand I probably *should* have told you to tell her, but I probably *would* have asked if you thought it might happen again or if you believed you could reign in those impulses from now on." He grimaces. "It's likely I would have told you to give yourself another chance. Most guys would."

Paulie looks at his lap. "Yeah, well, 'most guys' are exactly who I don't want to be."

"'Most guys' too ethically flexible for you?"

"I don't care what anyone else does, it's none of my business. I mean, it's all bullshit. I don't let my peers judge me, and I ain't ending up like my old man."

The bell rings; they walk to the door and watch the halls fill. "Got about five minutes before Period 8," Logs says. "You wanna grab something out of the lunchroom?"

"I'd like to grab Hannah out of the lunchroom." Paulie

pats his stomach, shakes his head. "Not hungry."

"If we're getting into open water you'll need to eat whether you're hungry or not."

"Gimme a day," Paulie says.

Logs grabs a brown paper bag from his top desk drawer and removes a small plastic container of green salad with ranch and four very small hard-salami-and-cheese-on-rye sandwiches. He extends one of the sandwiches toward Paulie. "Take it," he says. "For me."

Paulie laughs, grabs the sandwich, and halves it in one bite. "I mean it. I don't want to be my dad," he says. "At least not in that way. An affair about every year and a half, caught every time. Three weeks in an apartment or a motel, then back. Mom all hurt and shit but scared to lose him."

"I guess your folks are better parents than mates," Logs says. "Not good, but not all bad, either."

The first of the Period 8 kids saunter in, and Paulie clams up. He's been with some of these kids in P-8 for four years, and they've been through some intense discussions. Paulie is famous for making raw disclosures, but he does *not* feel like airing his shit with Hannah in this room. Not yet.

.2

"Hey, Tak," Arney Stack says as he rushes into Period 8, removing his jacket. "Heard you got taken out in the semis."

"Mr. Stack," Logs says. "Missed you in class this morning."

"Student council meeting," Arney says. "Didn't you get the memo from the office?"

Logs nods. He doesn't read office memos. Arney knows that.

Josh Takeuchi opens his lunch sack, which contains the first *real* lunch he's had since he started dropping weight at the beginning of wrestling season. "Yeah," he says, opening a ziplock bag containing three baloney sandwiches and two Snickers bars. "I got taken out in the semis."

"What happened? You went all the way to the finals last year," Arney asks.

"Yeah," Josh says, stuffing his mouth with the first sandwich. "I was sweating it this year, you know, having major doubts, and Firth told me to put it in the hands of the Lord."

Light laughter. "How'd that work for you?" Arney says.

"Not sure," Josh says back. "When I won the quarters I dropped to one knee and pointed to the heavens."

Marley Waits laughs out loud. "How'd *that* work for you?"

Ron Firth drops his forehead to the arm of his overstuffed chair.

"Again," Josh says, "not sure. I thought I was giving it up to the Lord but Terrence Davis was standing on the balcony right above me."

"Who's Terrence Davis?" Marley asks.

"The guy who kicked my ass in the semis," Josh says.

Firth looks up. "Do I have to do everything for you, Tak? You got to look where you're pointing, man."

"My Asiatic brother Tebowed up to his next opponent?" Justin Chenier says. "Damn!"

"You think this Davis guy intercepted it?" Bobby Wright asks.

Paulie closes his eyes and smiles. Literal Bobby.

"Actually, I think this Davis guy didn't care if I Tebowed him or not," Josh says. "All he cared about was how quick he could put my shoulder blades on the mat."

Ron Firth laughs. "You sure you dropped to the right knee? If you do it wrong, it's occult."

Josh just smiles and stuffs his face with the second sandwich. He points to his mouth. "Got a lot of catchin' up to do," he says, but all anyone hears are words passing through bread.

Logs wads his lunch sack and puts a three-pointer into the wastebasket. "So, what's up?" he says as the last of the Period 8 kids settle in, digging through backpacks and getting comfortable in desks and beanbags and old chairs Logs has hijacked over the past forty years on their way from the teachers' lounge to the Dumpster. *What's up?* is the way Logs starts every Period 8.

Any subject is fair game. No qualifications to enroll, no grade or credit, no attendance taken, but in a given year membership is consistent. There were years when Period 8 was the only reason Logs taught, when the educational philosophy du jour provided him almost no satisfaction; years when his personal life was in such a shambles he could barely bring himself to the classroom each day. But

Period 8 always brought him to life and grounded him. "I'm an old guy and you guys are young," he says at the start of every year. "But we have one common reference point: we're all as old as we've ever been. We all have history, and a future. History is known, the future not so much. My history is longer and hopefully my future shorter than yours. But we have the same challenge: to view what has happened to us in a way that influences what *will* happen."

Period 8 protocol: nobody gets hurt. Well, hurt maybe a little, but not injured.

"What's up is *this*," Hannah Murphy says.

Paulie can tell from her tone this is going exactly to the place he wants to avoid. Sweet Hannah. No prisoners.

"Hannah Murphy," Logs says. "Take it away."

"Are all men pigs?" she says.

Star lets herself into her empty house. Her dad is at work and her mother is collecting for the Junior League auction. She looks at her watch, thinks about school, shelves the thought. She'll catch up. She's always been able to catch up. She reaches to the bottom of her purse for a small pill, pops it, and starts running a tub in her bathroom.

• • •

"Are all men pigs," Logs says, scratching his chin. "Preamble to the male Bill of Rights, I believe. But methinks this question is loaded."

"Will a guy screw anything that makes itself available?"

"There may be exceptions in single-cell organisms," Logs says, "but if you stick with reptiles and mammals, you've got a pretty solid case."

Hannah glares toward Paulie, scowls, and looks away, back to Logs. "How are guys and girls supposed to trust each other, or more particularly, how are girls supposed to trust guys? I mean yeah, girls cheat, but it's got to be way more with guys."

Paulie slumps in his frayed easy chair. "Don't keep it general for me," he says to Hannah. "The half of this group that hasn't seen your Facebook page is now up to speed. This is P-8. Keep it real." He says it without sarcasm or spite.

Hannah shrugs. "Your call, superstar."

Discomfort bounces around the room. Nobody wants to mess with Hannah Murphy, but among the girls the news that Paulie Bomb is free isn't all bad.

"So. I cheated," Paulie says.

Justin's eyes narrow. "Ooooo." He looks at Hannah. "How'd you find out?"

"What difference does it make, Justin," Hannah says. "He cheated."

"The chick threaten you?" Justin says to Paulie. "Who was it? Maybe I got somethin' on her."

Paulie sighs. "Nobody threatened me. I cheated and I said so."

"To who?" Justin says. "You told somebody and they ratted you out?"

"I told *Hannah*," Paulie says. "Jeez."

Girls look at one another and then at Hannah. Guys look at one another and *not* at Paulie.

"Lemme get this right," Justin says. "You slipped up, didn't get caught, so you brought in friendly fire?"

Logs looks at the floor, slightly embarrassed. Justin sounds dangerously like *him*.

Paulie says, "Yup."

"Good thing you're not runnin' for ASB prez again," Justin says. "Don't think I could rally anyone behind you in the face of this. That just sounds, like, ill thought out."

At the end of his junior year, when Paulie made his failed run for the office of associated student body president, Justin, the self-proclaimed voice of people of color at Heller High, rallied his troops in support, but

Arney Stack carried the majority of voters nearly two to one. Paulie was cool, but Stack had an actual political agenda and a campaign staff.

Paulie smiles sadly over at Hannah. "Naw, man, it was completely thought out. You think I'd put myself in harm's way without thinking about it?"

Hannah is incredulous. "Can you believe this? Paulie Bomb cheats on his girlfriend, has the *huevos* to step up, and I'll bet ninety percent of the guys in this room think he's a pussy. Any of you chicks want to go lesbian with me? I mean, I'm liking the guy who cheated on me better than the ones who didn't, and I don't like him at *all*."

"I don't think he's a pussy," Bobby Wright says. It's vintage Bobby, barely audible.

"Nobody said he was a pussy," Justin says to Hannah. "I said he was stupid."

"Hard to see how you're helping me here, Jus," Paulie says.

"You sure aren't helpin' your*self*," Justin says back.

Hannah scans the room. "Okay, guys, show of hands. How many of you heroes have ever cheated on your girlfriend?"

No hands are raised.

"Duh!" she says. "Don't know why I thought I'd get truth out of a bunch of guys who think another guy's an idiot for fessing up. The praying mantis has it right, eat the guy's head off during conception and raise the kids on your own."

"Wait," Justin says. "I'll give you that some dudes aren't, like, Superman when it's about comin' clean, but it's not like we lie *all* the time. Fact, I'll bet ninety percent of our lies are just about sex."

"*That* makes it okay," Marley says.

"I'm just sayin, it's not like we lie just to lie. And chicks lie about sex, too."

"You're a math guy, Justin," Hannah says. "How do you think the two compare? Like right here at Heller, if you knew the total number of lies told about sex on any given day, think it would be fifty-fifty, boys and girls?"

Justin smiles. "Maybe not *fifty-fifty* . . ."

"Yeah," Hannah says. "Maybe not."

Paulie's jaw tightens. He wants *out* of this conversation. What happened was barely even about sex, but he started down that road back when he told Hannah, and he knows where it ends. "*Take me home, in fucking silence . . .*"

"It's not a fair fight, Murph," Justin says. "You took brother Logs's bio class."

"I don't know where you're going with this, Justin," Logs says.

"Stay with me. This shit is scientific."

"We're with you," Hannah says.

"This might sound a little crude . . ."

Hannah rolls her eyes.

". . . but guys're hard-wired, man. Look at dogs. You don't see some female dog breaking her chain and scaling a six-foot fence to get to a dude dog. But a Great Dane will ride across the river on the back of a dog-eatin' alligator to rub up against a Chihuahua in heat *knowin'* you can't put tab A into slot B. We do that shit 'cause there's no choice. You *never* catch me saying 'The devil made me do it.' *Darwin* made me do it."

Logs shakes his head, grateful that Period 8 kids seldom take these conversations home.

"Dude," Arney says. "Do you find it hard to keep a girlfriend?"

"Man, I've *always* got a girlfriend."

Paulie leans forward and touches his fingers to his toes, resting his head on his knees. "He means the *same* girlfriend, Jus."

"Yeah, well, see, that's the *point*," Justin says. "We're not doing this right. We're not doing it how we were *made*. You could make a case we're actually goin' against God's *law.*"

Ron Firth, the driving force behind *Youth for Christ* at Heller High, guffaws. "That would be a different law than *I* know. There's a way men and women are supposed to act."

"My point exactly," Justin says. "We're not men and women. We're *boys* and *girls.* Brain science guys say we're not cooked yet, remember, Brother Logs?"

"I do remember, Mr. Chenier, and I'm impressed that you understand all the wires may not be hooked up yet."

"No problem believin' that," Justin says. "Man, if I had to operate in this confusion the rest of my life, I'd take drugs."

Marley Waits's hard gaze connects with Hannah's and they execute their flawless synchronized eye roll. Marley says, "Every one of my mother's boyfriends—and they come in twos and threes—has a version of this very same song, though I have to say none of them so far is as funny as Justin Chenier." Marley has been a four-point plus student in every AP class Heller High School has offered and is, as she puts it, headed for the big time; her choice of most of the best universities in the country. "To put it in Hannah Murphy terms, what a bunch of happy horseshit."

"Maybe," Logs says, "but Justin's biology argument isn't a bad place to start." Logs waves a hand through the air, left to right. "How many of you have had some difficulty in relationships that you think has solely to do with the difference between male and female points of view?"

Students who have never even *had* a relationship raise their hands.

Paulie stands, stretches, moves toward the door. "I'm a little raw right now," he says. "I'll catch up with you guys tomorrow."

Hannah shakes her head in disgust. Arney smiles and watches Paulie go. His old buddy has never learned to play the game.

"Okay, folks," Logs says, "let's keep this civil." He nods toward Hannah, who shakes her head in mild disgust. "So where do we start? Justin, you were about to make a case why girls should give guys some leeway with their reptilian behavior."

"Not exactly how I was gonna put it," Justin says, "but yeah, there's driving force to consider."

"What you call 'driving force,' we call horny," Marley says.

"Sweet," says Heather Cole, a tough little freshman

cross-country runner. Hannah reaches across the aisle to high-five her.

"Call it nature," Justin says.

"So you think nature should trump your word?" Heather says.

"You shouldn't be trying to *get* our word. We're too young to be giving our word, at least for the long haul."

Josh Takeuchi finishes his last sandwich and stretches out on his beanbag. "Everything stays in the room, right?" Logs nods.

"'Cause I got a cool thing going with Sandra and I don't wanna get quoted out of context. . . ."

"Everything stays in the room," Logs says.

Tak turns to Hannah. "Soon as schools out, take your journalism recorder out on the street and ask every adult you pass if they're with the girl or boy they were with in high school."

Hannah says, "This is . . ."

"Naw, serious," Tak says. "We aren't made so we know exactly what to do. We gotta fuck up to find out."

"Brain science?" Marley says. There is a definite sarcastic tinge.

Tak shrugs. "I guess. I don't know what it's like for chicks, but when the circumstances are just right—or *wrong*—like when nobody's gonna find out . . . what can I say?"

"Maybe nothing more," Logs says. "Let's wrap this. Tell you what though, folks. These are questions you'll have to consider at some point, and the sooner the better. A good marriage counselor runs about a hundred-fifty an hour."

"You talkin' from experience?" Justin says.

"First time I went it was only fifty," Logs says.

"How'd it work?"

"I live with a cat."

.3

"I'm telling you, man, this might be too soon for you. It took me an hour to get feeling back into my hands." Paulie unloads his wetsuit from the back of the Beetle while Logs drags his from the bed of his Datsun pickup.

"Couldn't have you diving in and taking the easy way out," Logs says, "not after today's P-8."

"The easy way out?" Paulie gets it. "Oh, the *easy* way. Nah, I'd rather kill myself than commit suicide. This is a temporary situation that won't last more than fifteen, maybe twenty years."

"You're the Lou Gehrig of the water, my man," Logs says. "Seriously, though, you doing okay? Losing someone is no damn fun. And we're talking Hannah Murphy."

Paulie shakes talcum powder onto the inside of the wetsuit and over his body and chucks the container to Logs, who does the same. "I know, man," he says. "I just gotta trust that the universe didn't give me the best girl first. Hannah's cool, but . . ."

"But what?"

"But if it had been the other way around, if she'd cheated on me and then asked me, like, three or four times for a chance to explain, I'd have let her goddamn explain."

"You're pissed." Logs starts pulling on his suit. "Man, this is going to be cold."

"Yes, and yes," Paulie says. "And in just a second when we hit the water, none of this will matter." He adjusts his goggles.

They do hit the water and the air rushes out of Logs's lungs like he's a fireplace bellow. "You're right," he gasps, catching his wind. "I don't give a *damn* about your miserable life."

"Worst part's over," Paulie says after the water in their suits has approached body temperature. "Let's do it."

They swim out about the same distance Paulie swam earlier and turn parallel to the shore, treading as they set timers on their watches. "I'll take the first fifteen," Paulie says, "then you. We'll switch off and get the feel of it."

Both Paulie and Logs have put in monster indoor workouts during the winter and hit the weight room on off days. They have very different stroke patterns; Paulie's long and even, while Logs takes seven strokes to Paulie's five to make up for arm length and hand span. But they've been swimming together long enough that they fall into each other's pace automatically.

They swim eight fifteen-minute segments, four up and four back, switching sides every quarter hour so one keeps an eye on the shore while the other sets the pace. For the first three segments Paulie holds back, strength and size and youth all trump cards. But grit and tenacity and decades of experience even things out, and it's all either can do to stay with the other at the finish.

"Not bad for a first shot," Logs gasps, peeling off his wetsuit. He tiptoes barefoot to the passenger-side door, hauls out sweats and flip-flops.

"Man-oh-man, how do you do it? Are you really pushing sixty-five?" Paulie says. "No way should I be digging into my reserves to hang with you. Maybe I have fibromyalgia."

"Cute. Let's talk about a cure for that in the whirlpool,"

Logs says. "When my hands and feet start to thaw out I'll feel every one of those sixty-*four* years. Meet you up at the U."

In the pool area at the university student rec center, Paulie and Logs lower themselves into the otherwise unoccupied whirlpool, immersing to the neck with a mutual *aaahhhh* as the swirling, heated water envelops them. "Best part of swimming like that is stopping," Logs says. "I could give up the workouts, I just couldn't give up this."

"That's like saying I could give up setting myself on fire, if it didn't feel so good when they put me out."

"Addiction is an interesting phenomenon," Logs says. "What about you, feeling any better?"

Paulie smiles and sinks deeper, clear to his lower lip. "I can forget almost anything for a little while once I get in the water," he says, "but in the end I have to dry off. Man, Logs, I thought I should tell the truth, but fuck . . ."

"I know this doesn't mean a lot now, but time helps. Most of us can only feel shitty for so long."

"It doesn't help that I have to feel stupid, too," Paulie says. "It's not like I didn't know better. I mean, my old man . . . Jesus."

Logs grimaces.

"I was trying to get away, I swear. That sounds lame, but . . ."

"Much as I do not want to hear details, do you want to talk? Something feels really off about this, Paulie."

"Naw. This is too embarrassing."

Logs lays his head back and stares at the ceiling as Paulie takes a deep breath and sinks out of sight, letting the jets soothe his aching shoulder muscles. He holds his breath as long as possible, suspended just below the surface

When he comes up for air, Logs says, "You didn't hear any more about Mary Wells, by any chance."

"Why do you keep asking me about Mary Wells?"

"Same reason I ask about any kid I want the goods on. Four years you've been my mole. I've almost seemed cool, getting my information from you."

"I don't know much about Mary Wells. Everyone still calls her the Virgin Mary. Great grades . . . well, you know what kind of grades she gets. Doesn't go out with anyone who knows her dad and anyone who's been out with her once, knows her dad. What else is there to know?"

"The Virgin Mary, huh? That's kind of cruel."

"We're high school kids, Logs. Cruel's how we roll."

"But *you* don't call her that. . . ."

"No, Dad, I don't call her that."

"What I'm interested in," Logs says, "is where she is. She hasn't missed a class or a Period 8 in four years."

"Didn't Mrs. Byers call her house? Shit, I stop to get a drink outside the classroom three seconds after the bell and she thinks I'm going Ferris Bueller on her."

"I didn't report it," Logs says.

"Can't you get in trouble for that?"

"At this point I'll get in trouble only if I'm caught in bed with a dead girl or a live boy," Logs says. "I didn't report her because she stuck her head in my room after school a little while back, looking kind of desperate, and asked if I had time to talk. I had a pissed-off parent with me, so I asked her to wait. She looked like she'd been crying. Anyway, my meeting took longer than I expected and when it was over, she was gone. I tried to catch up with her the next day, but she blew me off like she'd never asked. A week later she doesn't show for class for the first time in her high school career. All her other classes are Running Start, here at the university. I don't know if she's making those or not."

"So why didn't you go ahead and mark her absent?"

Logs raises a water-wrinkled hand. "Swear to secrecy,"

he says. "We talk about her dad the same way you guys do. I don't know, I had this sense she was reaching out privately. If she's not here tomorrow, I'll do something."

Paulie says, "Nobody I know knows much about her other than that she's top-model good-looking and hard to get to know. Stack says he's studied with her a couple of times. She's kind of a mystery."

"She doesn't seem like Arney's type."

"Everybody was Arney's type when he was kicking my ass in that stupid election. He can get next to *any*body. Hell, *I* voted for him."

"The election's over."

Paulie laughs. "Arney's in campaign mode all the time. I gotta say, even being his halfway bud is a chore. He's just kind of, I don't know, always *working* it."

"Like . . ."

"I don't know. You just don't know what he's thinking."

Logs pulls himself out of the whirling, steaming water. "You think Arney knows something we don't?"

"All I know about Arney is what you see isn't always what you get." Paulie sinks deeper. "I've known him a long time. Once back in kindergarten his family was over at our place on Christmas night. I'd gotten this big-ass candy cane, like tall as me. I was saving it to show my friends. Arney gets all buddy-buddy with me, says we could eat it by ourselves and brag about it. That doesn't work so he goes Eddie Haskell on my mom, but she watches *Leave it to Beaver* reruns, too, so no go. We were playing around later in my room and he accidentally knocked it against the wall and it broke. After I stopped bawling and threatening to kill him it was, you know, what the hell, we might as well eat it. We unwrapped it and he took a big ol' chunk and . . . I don't know, there was this look on his face like . . . he'd known he'd get it all along."

Logs shakes his head. "It stuck with you. That was a long time ago."

"Well, I've seen that look a few times since." He doesn't mention he saw it recently, just before he fucked up.

"Listen, I gotta get out of here before somebody has to slap my chest with the shockers," Logs says. "Catch you tomorrow."

"Later."

Hannah hits "Save" on her Word document, sets her laptop to the side of the bed, and wanders downstairs to the kitchen for a snack. Her arms and shoulders are tight from her afternoon workout at the gym on the ergonomic rowing machine, even though she's in perfect condition for this time of year. She cranked it extra-hard today, her anger at Paulie and the dumb-ass guys in Period 8 and the faceless girl Paulie cheated with driving her. If she could find *that* girl, there would be a short, loud, threatening meeting of the minds.

Maybe all's fair in love and war, she thinks, *but chicks* have *to have solidarity, or guys will . . . well,* look *what guys will do.* The refrigerator light spills into the darkened kitchen as she removes the carton of milk and a half loaf of wheat bread and lays them on the granite counter. She leaves the refrigerator door open long enough to dig the peanut butter jar from a corner of the cupboard, open it, and spread the contents thickly onto the bread. She pours a glass of milk, returns the bread and milk to the fridge, and eats in pitch-dark.

She fumes, alternating between thoughts of screwing every guy friend Paulie ever had and kicking the ass of every girl who ever stole another girl's boyfriend. It's going to be one of those nights: forty-five minutes of fitful sleep followed by sledgehammer wake-up and thoughts of grave malice, then chest-crushing loss. It's easy to appear tough in public, more difficult to pull it off in the silence of loneliness. Paulie was a soul mate. And he was *hot*. She loved watching him pull his dripping body onto the dock when the water warmed enough that he got rid of that stupid wetsuit. She loved eating pizza and talking about sports and what a drag high school was getting to be and going off to college and taking chances. There are just no other guys like Paulie. She misses him desperately, but she *will* miss him because she is *not* going back to that. All his talk about not being like his dad. . . .

For the past two years, as soon as the water turned warm enough, Hannah would bring her single scull to the lake with Paulie and Mr. Logs and guide them the mile and a half across, the two of them swimming on either side. Then she would throw out abbreviated water-ski ropes that attached to the sides of her scull and pull them back while Paulie whined "Are we there yet?" or counted like a coxswain, or in some other way annoyed her. On good days they'd do it twice.

Later the three would go for pizza, or if Mr. Logs begged off, she and Paulie would take a pizza to a makeshift "apartment" that doubled as storage space above a vacant storefront at a strip mall near Paulie's house. If a small Wonder Woman refrigerator magnet was not placed discreetly over the keyhole, they would use their key, put Wonder Woman in her place to remind any of the six other key holders it was first-come, first-serve, and slip inside.

In the dim, warm safety of that space, to the music-of-choice emanating from the iPod dock, or a favorite movie on the 23-inch flat screen the shareholders had thrown in matching dollars on, Hannah could let down and be Hannah.

"I cheated" ended all that.

She pulls on a pair of sweatpants and a hoodie, slips her feet into her flip-flops, doesn't bother to tell her parents where she's going, or *that* she's going, and walks to her car.

"Can I come in?" Hannah stands on Logs's porch, staring at him in the doorway. He's dressed almost exactly as she is.

"Hannah. Of course. What are you doing out at this hour?"

She sits on the couch, kicks off the flip-flops, and curls her feet under.

Logs says, "Something to drink?"

"What I want to drink, you'd get fired for giving me."

Logs sits in his recliner, hits Mute on the remote. "Talk to me."

"I've got a rule," she says. "I just don't put up with that shit."

"It's a good rule."

"So why do I feel so bad?"

"You guys seemed to be a pretty good match."

"You know who the chick was?" she asks.

Logs shakes his head. "Couldn't tell you if I did."

She points a finger at him. "*Wouldn't* tell me if you did. Man code, right?"

"Human code," Logs says back. "It would be the same if it were you instead of him."

"Man, I will find her and I will kick her ass," Hannah says.

"Girl code?"

"I hate this whole dating thing, or boy-girl thing or whatever you want to call it. You're never safe. I mean, if Paulie Bomb is a player, who is there? And why—"

"You know," Logs interrupts, "as much as it might sound like bull, Justin Chenier had a point today. I don't think Paulie's a player, but biology is a powerful thing. We have to learn to out*think* it, I guess. If I ran the zoo, people would wait on sex, but I don't run the zoo and sex happens when it happens. I settle for good decisions about birth and STD control. Since I *can't* change God's faulty mind-body engineering, I might lobby for a different standard for 'cheating.'"

Hannah is visibly irritated. "Meaning?"

"Meaning sex and love go together sometimes and sometimes they don't. I get that you guys made a promise to each other and Paulie broke it. I'm not letting him off the hook, but something he said makes me believe there are extenuating circumstances. If I felt the pull as strongly as you seem to feel it, I'd make sure I knew *everything* before going zero tolerance."

Hannah stares at her lap. "No offense, Mr. Logs, but that sounds like manspeak, which sounds exactly the same as horseshit."

"Hey," Logs says, "if this relationship stuff were easy, more people would do it right." He sighs. "And by the way, almost *no*body gets it right the first time."

Hannah touches her chest. "It's this *hurt,*" she says. "If I could just . . ." She snaps back. "There are certain things I can't have in my life, and my boyfriend screwing other chicks is one of them. How could Paulie not *get* that? My god, look at his *parents*."

Logs sighs again. "Tell me what I can do for you, Hannah."

She starts to speak, hesitates. "Listen to me bitch, I guess."

"That I can do."

"And keep your mouth shut. You can't tell Paulie I was here and you can't tell him I give a shit."

"You get the same confidentiality he gets," Logs says. "Just let me know when you want advice."

"I want advice! *Jesus,* Mr. Logs. Quit treating me like I'm some kind of grown-up. Why do I have to pretend like *my* brain's developed any more than those jerkoffs? AAUGH!"

Logs smiles. "Look, you don't have to sleep with Paulie to find out if you can still be friends. Start working out with us again. It's always better to swim with a boat and not have to look for the shore all the time. You said it'll be three or four weeks before your new scull is ready. By then maybe this will look different."

"If I went with you guys now, I'd hit him on the head with an oar."

"This doesn't sound like some guy who waited for his girlfriend to go out of town so he could try someone new. Something is unusual about this."

"Yeah, right. Some—"

"Let it sit, Hannah. Most things look different with time and distance."

On the porch, Hannah says, "Thanks, Mr. Logs. I'll bet a bunch of girls had a hard time hating *your* guts back in your time."

"Not as hard as you might think," Logs says. "Paulie is twice the man I was."

"Yeah, well, we'll see." She starts down the stairs.

"Hey, one other thing."

Hannah stops.

"You know anything about Mary Wells?"

"The Virgin Mary?"

Logs sighs. "Yeah. Mary Wells."

"Not much. I mean, what's to know? You couldn't be much more obscure than Mary Wells for someone as pretty as she is."

"Have you seen her around?"

"She's Running Start. I wouldn't."

"I know, but she's been in Period 8 every day for nearly

four years and suddenly she's gone. Missing government, too. Last time I saw her she seemed distressed."

"I hadn't noticed," Hannah says. "If someone told me Mary Wells seemed 'distressed,' I wouldn't even know what that would look like. She's, like, a smiley *mannequin*. I mean, get a personality, girl. Sic Mrs. Byers on her."

Logs waves her away. "Nah. I'll follow up tomorrow. You drive safe, okay?"

"Thanks, Mr. Logs."

Hannah disappears into the dark of the driveway.

.4

Logs pops a beer and walks back into the living room, punching Power on the remote, watching the oversized flat screen go black. The porch light casts warm stripes through the half-closed venetian blinds and he sits, insulated from school and the world. Lessons are planned, most of the town sleeps, nothing or no one but his cat, Gehrig, to talk with until morning. *This is it.* He won't let himself go fallow, will swim with Paulie, or by himself when Paulie leaves. He'll travel; maybe write. There was a time back in his twenties when he thought he could be a writer, maybe even as a living. But story after story, great idea after great idea, died in mid-telling. He simply didn't know how to end any of them. *Maybe now,* he thinks, *when I'm closer to my own ending, when I understand endings better.*

He feels the light, acrobatic pressure of cat feet in his lap, takes a long swig of his beer, and strokes the tiny cat's head. Gehrig is fifteen, can't weigh more than six pounds. Black with white bib and mittens, long and lean as a javelin, this cat has been hit by a car, lost a chunk of shoulder to some neighborhood marauding animal, spent several nights locked in a neighbor's shed, and, like his namesake, never missed a day (except for those locked in the shed) as Logs's companion. He calls Gehrig and Gehrig comes. Like a dog. He's hunted birds of his equal weight and left their remains on the living room rug as presents with maddening regularity.

Now Gehrig lies stretched like a tiny afghan across Logs's legs, purring like logging equipment. His entire head fits in the cup of Logs's hand and he massages between the ears to increasing vibrating decibels. "We've had a good run, don't you think, buddy?" Logs asks. "Fixed more than we broke, maybe? Lent a hand up?"

Gehrig's answer is his steady purr.

Hannah drives the back road home, deliberately avoiding city streets and forcing herself to concentrate. She's got at least another hour of homework and it's closing in on midnight. She pulls to the side of the road and screams "FUUUUUCK!" at the top of her lungs, pounding her fists against the steering wheel. Then she takes a deep breath and pulls back onto the blacktop.

It's only a few more miles to her house on this winding two-lane, but it's starting to feel like a hundred, her eyelids drooping under the weight of crushing fatigue. Not much chance with homework tonight; maybe she can get up early enough to catch up. Or maybe charm someone into letting her copy. She punches the power knob on her satellite radio, cranks up the volume, and hops from station to station looking for the old stuff. The really old stuff. *Logs* old. She regularly torments friends and enemies alike singing lyrics to songs written at the very birth of rock and roll. Now she wails along, loud to keep herself awake and off-key because that's her only choice:

Where oh where could my baby be . . .

She reaches for the volume to crank it even louder, looks up barely in time to veer around a B-movie apparition, a girl with flowing dark hair in a long white coat.

"What the hell?" She checks her rearview mirror, sees nothing, speeds about a hundred feet to a wide spot and flips a U-turn.

The girl's back comes into view, but she doesn't turn, walks straight down the middle of the road. Hannah pulls up beside her, rolls down the side window. "Hey!"

The girl stops, peers into the car.

"Mary?" Hannah says.

Mary Wells sways, stares straight at her. "Hannah Murphy?"

"Yeah. Are you okay? What are you doing out here? It's almost midnight."

"I know, I'm just . . . I'm . . ."

"Where's your car? You need a ride?"

"My car." Mary glances around. "Yeah, I guess I do need a ride."

"Get in. I'll take you home."

Mary looks at the door handle, doesn't move. Hannah unhooks her seat belt, reaches over, and opens the door. Mary gets in, leans back against the seat and closes her eyes. "Thanks. Not home, though."

"Where, then?"

"Oh, God, I don't know."

"It's *midnight,* Mary, I've got to take you someplace."

"I know." She pushes her palms against her forehead. "I know. Someplace."

Hannah waits. "*My* place," she says finally.

With face in hands, Mary nods.

"Seat belt," Hannah says, but Mary doesn't move. Hannah reaches around her and pulls the belt across Mary's chest. "Just close your eyes, I'll have you there in a minute."

Moments later they pull in front of a modern split-level. Hannah helps Mary into the dark house, leads her by the elbow into the guest room adjacent to hers, helps her partially undress and gets her under the covers, pausing only to yell back to her dad that everything is fine and she'll talk with him in the morning. Hannah has a million questions of which she asks none. She has *never* seen Mary like this. This is the Virgin Mary. Mary Wells is *bubbly.*

As Hannah starts to leave, Mary clutches her forearm. "Thanks," she says. "Really."

"It's okay," Hannah says. "Get some sleep; you look . . . just go to sleep."

Mary's eyes close.

Only hours earlier, Paulie throws his workout gear into a corner of his room, kicks the door shut, and sprawls facedown across the bedspread, dog tired from two long workouts and the weight of his first day without Hannah. He was in Period 8 with her and he's seen her in the halls, but is no longer allowed to punch her lightly on the shoulder or put his arms around her waist from behind. Somebody else . . . he can't think about that.

He answers a knock on his bedroom door with, "Yeah?"

"It's me, Paul. I've eaten, but there's plenty left over. Want me to warm it up?"

"I'm good, Mom. I grabbed a burger with Jus and Arney."

"You need more than a burger, honey. You did two workouts today. You know how that cold water saps you."

"'A burger' is a figure of speech. I ate three. Fries. Shake. I'm good."

"You need your vegetables."

She is not going away. This is not about dinner. "Ketchup, Mom. I had ketchup. It's a vegetable. Since the Reagan administration. Read about it last year in U.S. history."

"That was disallowed. And we're Democrats," Lilly Baum says through the door. "Ketchup is not a vegetable."

Paulie sighs and pushes himself up, walks over, and opens the door. "You win, Mom. Raw vegetable platter.

Lots of ranch. Give me five minutes. Dad come over?"

Lilly closes her eyes and shakes her head.

Shit. A raw-vegetables-with-ranch counseling session.

"Okay," he says. "Five minutes. Lots of ranch."

At the table Paulie opens a bottle of Gatorade and scoops the ranch out of a bowl with a stick of celery. "I thought Dad was coming over so you guys could talk."

His mom looks away. "He had to work late."

"Which you don't believe." *I just* saw *him and he was looking forward to coming over.* Paulie *does* hate knowing so much, but he also hates waiting for the hurt to leak out of his mother drip by drip. Time constraints alone make that a huge pain in the ass.

"I don't know, Paul. I don't know what to believe anymore. Listen, let's do something nice as a family tomorrow, whether your father comes over or not. Why don't you invite Hannah for dinner and we'll get a movie or something. You two can pick."

Shit. This is not the time to tell his mother that Hannah won't be coming to dinner tomorrow or any other night, because he did exactly what *she* thinks his dad is doing right now. "Hannah's buried in school stuff," he says. "She waited too long to get her college applications in and she's busting her butt to get her essays written." It isn't a total lie. Hannah *is* behind on her college applications. "Mom," he says, "you're not even forty. You work out; you barely look thirty and you'll probably live to be at least eighty-five. This isn't even halftime. You already have a perfect son."

His mother smiles.

"Dad is who he is. Unless he has a stroke or somethin' he's not going to change. End this. You'd like each other a lot better." He takes a deep breath. *Man, who am I to be giving anybody advice?*

His mother smiles again and touches his arm. "Maybe you're right, Paul. It's just . . . so hard to let go."

Paulie looks at his watch. 8:30. He needs to get away. No Rocket shift tonight. Arney and Justin might still be at open gym. He's tired, but not tired enough to put himself into the coma it will take to get a good night's sleep on *this* night.

Paulie drops his workout bag onto the bleachers and watches Justin and Arney and several other guys he knows finish a five-on-five full-court pickup game. Jus and Arney play on opposite teams, guarding each other fiercely; it's an even match. Both are strong and in good shape and what they lack in skill they make up in passion. Paulie finishes lacing up his shoes as Justin drives on Arney, spins and goes for the layup. As Justin stretches for the hoop, Arney undercuts him and Justin crashes onto his shoulder blades. All play halts at the sickening sound of bone on hardwood. After a fleeting hesitation Arney drops to his knees beside Justin, apologizing profusely. "Shit, man, I couldn't stop. You okay? Hey, buddy, you okay?"

Justin lies there a few seconds, checking for damage. "Yeah, I'm okay. Watch that, man, you're gonna kill someone."

Arney brings the ball in on the next play and his guy drains a jumper, ending the game. Fist bumps, butt slaps all around. Almost. Justin walks away from Arney.

Arney spots Paulie, jogs over, and sits. "Been here since six," he says. "Shoulda come earlier, we could have used you."

"Swam this afternoon," Paulie says. "Then had to check in at home. You guys up for a little two-on-one?"

"Hey, Justin!" Arney hollers. "Stay awhile and school the Bomb? Man, I'm sorry about that undercut."

Justin looks up from the drinking fountain, twists his shoulders, and stretches. "Never too late to school the Bomb," he yells back.

They shoot around long enough for Paulie to warm up, then line up at the top of the key to shoot for first outs. Arney swishes his first shot and the other two miss.

"Make it, take it," Justin says. "Every bucket counts two, first free throw two, one after that. Score five, shoot free throws 'til you miss or hit five in a row and take it out. Game to twenty-one." Standard cutthroat rules.

Arney shoots a three that deflects off the back rim in a high arc out to Justin, who drives to the hoop, right at Paulie. He goes for the layup, sees Paulie towering over him, pumps, switches hands, and attempts to force it from his off side. Paulie slaps the ball into the bleachers.

"Damn!"

"Don't bring that weak shit in here," Paulie says.

While the two trash-talk, Arney retrieves the ball and slides in for a layup.

Justin still jaws at Paulie. "Whose shit you callin' weak? After that sorry show you put on in P-8 today?"

"It *wasn't* my best 'man-up' hour."

"You couldn't pick a best *minute* outta that hour."

Paulie backs Justin into the key, protecting the ball with his body. When Arney tries to sneak around to slap the ball out, Paulie crosses over and swishes a short hook.

"Man, you are messin' with my stereotype. How is some tall pale *distance swimmer* scorin' over me?"

"*Over* you isn't exactly high," Paulie says, dribbling to the top of the key.

"All I can say is you should have listened better in kindygarten," Justin says. "Got to make good choices, man."

Arney slaps the ball out of Paulie's hand, steps back, and drops a perfect three. "I love playing with you guys," he says. "While you go at each other, I just wait for *opportunity*."

"How's *that* fit with your stereotype?" Paulie says to Justin. "It's one thing to get schooled by a tall pale merman, a whole 'nother thing to get spanked on the court by the ASB prez. You know how a guy *gets to be* student body president? By sucking at everything else."

"Funny," Arney says. "Hey, you guys, I gotta go. Sorry about your, uh, dilemma, Paulie. Maybe if you sit back and be cool things'll work out."

"Bet if you just told her who it was, it'd be all good," Justin says. "Let her take it out on the chick."

"Yeah, and be accessory to a felony," Paulie says back.

"Maybe you should tell *us*," Justin says. "We could leak it."

Arney says, "There's an idea."

"I'm not tellin' *you* guys anything."

Arney pulls on his sweats. "Thought you always told the truth." He smiles. "So . . . tell us the truth."

"I am," Paulie says. "The truth is, I'm not telling you."

Arney waves over his shoulder as he exits the gym, while Paulie and Justin go one-on-one until the lights blink.

Logs pulls into the teacher's parking lot after second period the next morning, having taken two hours of sick leave for dental work, and spots three police cars parked out front, two more than he would expect. In the front office he finds the regularly assigned school officer along with two others engaged in conversation with Marj Johannsen, the principal.

Dr. Johannsen looks up as Logs enters. "Mary Wells is missing."

"From school?" It's a dumb question.

"Missing," Dr. Johannsen says. "This is Officer Rankin," she says, pointing to the taller of the two unfamiliar officers. "He says she's been gone two days. Her father reported it early this morning. The police are asking if we can get some students to help search the county park near the Wells's house."

"They're thinking foul play?"

"Mr. Wells reports that her room was torn up; a bookcase overturned, bedcovers on the floor," Officer Rankin says. "He says she normally keeps an immaculate room, and no way is his girl a runner." He nods at Dr. Johannsen. "I'm hearing she has a promising future."

"She does have that," Logs says. "You say she's been gone two days?"

"That's what he says."

"And he just reported it today?"

Officer Rankin only raises his eyebrows. "We have people over there now, but there's not a lot to go on. The room has been straightened up."

"What? That doesn't sound right."

Officer Rankin shrugs. "There's a lot doesn't sound right. That house has better security than City Hall. Nobody heard anything that sounded like struggle." He shakes his head. "Chief says we treat it at face value, so we're gonna look. Short window of time here if there *is* foul play."

Logs turns to Marj. "What can I do?"

"I thought maybe your lunch period kids would be best," Marj says. "They all know her and most of them could afford to miss a half day. It will take us until lunch to get parental permission and get a bus over here anyway.

You could ride out with them and I'll get a sub to cover your afternoon classes. Officer Rankin says there will be personnel at the park to meet you and organize."

"Sounds good." Logs waits until the police have finished making arrangements and are walking toward the exit before saying more. "This *is* strange, right?" he says when the doors at the end of the hall slam shut.

"I thought so too. I mean, had there been more evidence than a torn-up room, and only a *reported* torn-up room at that, I could see combing the park."

"You say that to Officer Rankin?"

She nods. "He said 'Orders from the chief,' that people like Mr. Wells have a much better chance of getting quick action than the run-of-the-mill citizen."

"Well, I think something doesn't add up, but I'm not a cop."

"I've called the Wells house several times, but there's no answer. I left messages on both cells. I'm skeptical about providing students to search but better safe than sorry, I suppose. Rankin seemed to think it's urgent. It would be awful if we refused and they found her in there." She shudders. "Supposedly there's a rapidly closing window following a disappearance and we're well over twenty-four hours already. KXLY is on their way, which I'm not real happy about since we've had no contact with Mary's parents. I think I'll refer them to the police."

The bus pulls up in front of the school and the Period 8 kids board. Paulie approaches Logs from behind. "Could I talk to you?"

"Can it wait?" Logs says. "We need to get this bus moving as quick as we can."

"Yeah," Paulie says, "it can wait. But not too long, okay?"

"You got it, buddy. Soon as I get a chance to breathe, we're talking. This is crazy."

"Yeah. Maybe crazier than you think."

"Couldn't be."

Justin comes up behind Paulie and bulls him onto the bus. "Let's get this show on the road."

"Catch you on board," Paulie yells over his shoulder.

.5

Hannah brakes her car at the south end of the county park and jumps out. She fell asleep after putting Mary Wells to bed last night, woke up, hit the snooze button on her clock four times, and then put it on permanent snooze against the far wall, forgetting momentarily that Mary was in the next room. Except when she finally got up and checked, Mary wasn't.

Logs stands talking with a police officer, surrounded by several students who have been searching. She insinuates herself between them. "Mr. Logs, can I talk with you? In private?"

"Hey, Hannah. What about?"

"About Mary Wells."

"Mary Wells is who we're talking about," Logs says. "You can talk in front of Officer Rankin."

"Mrs. Byers said Mary's been missing two days."

"That's right."

"I saw her last night."

The officer says, "Where? When?"

"After I left your house, Mr. Logs, just after midnight. I picked her up in the middle of the road."

Officer Rankin eyes Hannah, then Logs. "She was at your house at *midnight*? I was under the impression—"

"We were discussing—"

"Oh, for Christ sake!" Hannah says. "I'm eighteen years old. If I want to fuck my teacher—"

Logs interrupts. "And tell the nice man you don't."

Hannah breathes deep. "Mary Wells has not been missing for two days. She was asleep in our guest room eight hours ago."

"Her father said—"

"I don't care what her father said. Her father's the reason she's scared of everything. Everybody knows that."

Rankin removes his hat and scratches his head. "I'm sure Mr. Wells will be happy with this news. You're sure it was Mary."

Hannah looks at him like he's an idiot. "I picked her up, drove her home, and put her to bed. It was Mary."

"So where is she now?"

"When I got up this morning she was gone," Hannah says, and shrugs.

"Did she say where she'd been?" Rankin squints, palms up. "Her dad hasn't seen her for a while."

"No, she didn't," Hannah says. "She seemed so out of it, I didn't ask questions. She sure didn't want me taking her home."

"Out of it how?"

Hannah gives him the same look. "Out of it like she didn't want to go home."

Logs looks at Rankin. "What do you think?"

"I'll call Mr. Wells."

"What about the search?"

"Let me talk with Wells," Rankin says. "I'm not calling anything off until I know more." He walks toward his patrol car.

"What a dick," Hannah says. "I just told him she's not missing. What, he has to hear it from an adult?"

"He's a cop," Logs says. "He has to be sure. He doesn't know you, Hannah, and thanks to you he may have some suspicion that you're sleeping with your government teacher who is at least old enough to be your grandfather."

"He's still a dick," Hannah says.

Logs smiles. Hannah Murphy is a reasonable young lady most of the time, but when she's not, she's *not*. "Tell me what happened."

"I was driving home, the back way like I said. I was sleepy so I rolled down the window and was messing with the radio when I looked up and saw this, like, *apparition*. Mr. Logs, I almost hit her. She had to see me coming, I was the only car on the road and she was like, straddling the yellow line. She just looked up, all . . . *vacant*."

"What did she say?"

"I asked if she wanted a ride home, was ready to offer her an alibi if she needed one. I mean, everyone knows her dad. Mary Wells could go out every night with a different guy if they all didn't worry that the evening would end in their death."

Logs watches Rankin sitting in his patrol car, one leg in and one out, talking on his police radio. "Maybe a little exaggeration?"

"A little, not much. The only guy I know who's not afraid of him is Arney. Anyway, she did *not* want to go home but she didn't have another idea. I mean, I could barely get her to talk. It was like she was on something. So I took her home with me." She smiles. "Paying it forward. Who knows when I'll need a hideout again? Anyway, when I woke up this morning I forgot she was there and decided to catch a little more sleep. Like, what am I going to learn in government?"

"You're a funny girl."

"When I remembered, I went into the guest room and it was empty."

"You said the only guy not afraid of her dad is Stack?"

"Yeah, he says he's taken Mary for coffee a couple of times. Walks right up to the door and starts a conversation. Mr. Wells treats him different than other boys. At least that's what Arney says."

"Arney's a politician," Logs says.

"Arney's fearless," Hannah says back. "Or crazy."

As she says it, Arney walks up. "Hey, Hannah, how strange is this?"

"Stranger than you think," Hannah says. "I was with Mary last night."

Arney looks bewildered. "Last night? That's not . . ." He starts to walk away, turns back. "When?"

"Near midnight," Hannah says. "I almost ran her down. She was way zoned out, walking down the middle of the road. . . ." Hannah finishes her story much as she gave it to Logs.

"Wow, that doesn't sound like Mary. You took her home?" He looks at students coming out of the woods. "So how does all *this* happen?"

"My home, not hers," Hannah says. "What's the matter with you, Arney? You think I'm making this up?"

"No, no," he says, shaking his head. "Just doesn't sound like Mary, that's all."

"Well, she may very well be missing from *her* place for two days," Hannah says, "but she isn't *gone*. And like I said, she was whack."

"What did she say?"

"That she didn't want to go home."

"Why would she not want to go home?"

"She's *Mary Wells*, Arney. Would you want to go home if your dad was Mr. Wells? I don't even know her dad's first name, unless it's *Mister*."

"His name is Victor," Arney says. "And he's not such a bad guy if you don't let him intimidate you. Shoot, I've been out with Mary."

"You guys have been *out* out?"

"A few times," Arney says. "A movie, whatever."

"A movie," Hannah says. "*Little Mermaid*?"

Arney shakes his head. "Her situation isn't as bad as everybody thinks. Most of that stuff is rumor."

"Yeah, right."

Arney turns to Mr. Logs. "So we calling this off?"

"Officer Rankin is on the phone with Mr. Wells now," Logs says. "They'll give us direction soon." He turns to Hannah. "Can you remember anything else?"

"No. I should have asked more questions, I guess." She looks up to see Arney next to the police car, talking with Officer Rankin. She laughs. "Arney has to be in the middle of *everything*."

A Lexus pulls into the parking lot. The driver's-side door flies open and Victor Wells steps out. Officer Rankin approaches him from the patrol car and they exchange quick words, then approach Hannah.

Rankin says, "Victor Wells, this is . . . I'm sorry, young lady, I didn't get your name."

"Hannah. Murphy."

"Nice to meet you," Mr. Wells says. He doesn't extend his hand. "Officer Rankin here says you claim to have been with my daughter last night. Might I ask why it took you so long to say so?"

Wells is a tall man, well over six feet, and athletic. Hannah stiffens. "I don't *claim* to have been with her. I *was* with her."

Wells looks Hannah up and down. "What time was that?"

Rankin says, "I told you, sir, around—"

Wells holds up a hand. "I want to hear it from the young lady."

"I found her around midnight. She was walking on the road."

"And what were you doing out at that time on a school night?"

Logs takes a deep breath, closes his eyes.

"You know," Hannah says, "drinking, smoking dope, looking for cheap, easy sex."

"Young lady, do you think this is funny?"

"I think," Hannah says, "that it's none of your business what I was doing out that late and if you want to know about Mary, you should ask me about Mary."

Wells glares at Rankin, who shrugs.

"I'm sorry," he says to Hannah. "I've been upset. Did

my daughter tell you anything that might help us find her?"

"I offered her a ride home, but she didn't want to go, and I'm probably breaking a confidence here, but it was because of you."

"She has *no* reason—"

Hannah gestures surrender. "She didn't want to go home. The rest of it is none of *my* business. She was kind of, like, *disoriented*, and not all that informative. I took her to my house. When I got up this morning she was gone. I thought she'd gone to school, then I heard on the news she was missing."

"Nothing else was said?"

"Well, I offered her an alibi."

"Excuse me?"

"You know," Hannah says, "an excuse for being gone; 'course I didn't know she'd been gone this long."

"Why in the *world* would you do that?"

"To keep her out of trouble," Hannah says. She glances over at Logs. *Sheesh. Is this guy a mammal?*

"I guess that's what passes for loyalty these days," Wells says.

"Actually," Logs says, "that passes for loyalty in *any* days."

"You're sure it was my daughter. Mary."

"I've gone to school with her for four years," Hannah says.

"She's never mentioned you."

"Until today I probably haven't mentioned her. I didn't say we were friends, I said we've gone to school together."

"I suppose there's no reason to believe you're not telling the truth."

"I could be personality disordered," Hannah says.

Wells ignores her.

"We need to call off the search," Officer Rankin says. "Mr. Logsdon, could you help us call these kids back to the bus? I'll catch up with your principal. You all might be able to actually get some education in today."

Hannah slugs Logs's shoulder. "That would make it different from *most* days, huh, Teach?"

"You make it hard to defend America's youth sometimes, little girl." To the officer, he says, "Yeah, I can get these kids rounded up and back to the learning factory." He punches speed dial on his cell to let Dr. Johannsen know they're coming back, then goes to round everyone up.

Logs walks toward Victor Wells, who's now standing next to his car. "Mr. Wells, how can I help? Obviously your daughter hasn't been abducted, but you still don't know where she is. I've been worried about her lately; she's not been in my noon gathering."

Mary's father regards Logs warily. "I have to tell you, Mr. Logsdon, I'm not a fan of your 'noon gathering.'"

"I can't say I'm surprised."

"It's elements like—what do you call it, eighth period?—that put ideas into kids' heads that come to this." He waves his hand over the parking lot and the students now returning.

"You think my Period 8 is to blame for you and your daughter's troubles?"

"What makes you think my daughter and I are having trouble?"

"Obstinate as she can be, Hannah Murphy doesn't make things up. Your daughter's gone, she has to know you're worried, and she isn't doing a thing to alleviate that worry. In my book that indicates trouble. Look, Mr. Wells, it's none of my business what goes on in anybody's home, if it isn't abuse, other than how it affects a student in school. I've had Mary in one class or another since she was a freshman. She's been a phenomenal student and for the life of me, before this last week I can't remember her missing a class. Forgive me, but when I see a perfect student drop over the edge, I figure there's a lot I don't know. So, if there's anything I can do to help, I'm offering it."

Mr. Wells's expression softens. "I appreciate that, Mr. Logsdon, but I'm afraid the kind of help you have to offer in this situation isn't really help."

"Suit yourself, sir. The offer stands."

"*That* was an interesting way to start the day." Justin Chenier leans back in his seat across the aisle from Paulie and looks out the bus window. "Look at Arney," he says. "Gettin' all friendly with the cops now."

"Crazy, Hannah finding Mary wandering around in the middle of the night," Paulie says. "You talk to her?"

"Shit no," Justin says. "I think she's still pissed at me for the other day in Logs's lunchtime extravaganza."

"Naw, Hannah's not like that. She'll be pissed at me forever, but you can *say* any shit you want to her."

"Just got to be careful what you *do*, huh?"

"Exactly."

Justin shakes his head. "Whew. Guy like Wells hollers, folks come runnin'. He's a strange one."

"He's not as strange as everyone makes him out to

be," Arney says, plopping in the seat next to Justin. "A little uptight, maybe, but he's a pretty cool guy if you get to know him."

"Yeah, but Arney," Paulie says, "room's messed up big time. She's gone two days and *then* he reports her missing, but meanwhile the room gets cleaned? Come on, man. I'll bet Mary Wells hasn't spent three nights away from home since third grade. Think about it: she's wandering around all fucked up at midnight, he doesn't, like, check with the school or any of us, then runs to the cops hollering foul play."

"Right on," Justin says, "and by the way, we're still missin' a virgin."

"That we are," Arney says. "That we are."

.6

After school, Paulie heads for the lake. Logs may come later, but he's buried in teachers' meetings and a damage-control local news conference.

Paulie lays his wetsuit out on the dock, thinking about Hannah and Mary Wells and how his life has taken a turn for the bizarre. A paraphrased H. L. Mencken quotation he has taped to his bedroom wall pops into his head: "For every complex question there's a simple answer— and it's wrong." He thinks too about *All the Pretty Horses,* a novel he read in English this year. The main character, John Grady Cole, says, "There ain't but one truth. The truth is what happened." There was a time when Paulie thought it was as simple as that: learn the truth and tell it.

It started with a Sunday school lesson back in elementary school, one taught by a kind of hippie throwback youth minister who believed finding the truth and exposing it was Jesus's *modus operandi*. You wouldn't tell some poor kid that you recognized the shirt he was wearing because it used to belong to you, or chide someone for some other reality that could only hurt. But with the big things, the things that bore *consequence*, well, you told it; you told what happened. But as he gets ready to hit the water, Paulie thinks it's a little more complicated than that. He told Hannah *what happened*. She didn't want to hear more. *What happened* was all she needed to bring the curtain down on what Paulie had considered the best thing that ever *happened* to him. Hannah knew how Paulie felt about his father's wanderings, about the hours upon hours he'd sat listening to his mom. She was there the night his mother went totally off and broke nearly every breakable thing in the kitchen—dishes, glasses, CorningWare—packed a suitcase, and stormed out.

"Guess she's finally had it," Hannah had said, holding Paulie's hand as they stared at the carnage.

"It just means a new set of dishes," Paulie had replied. "This time tomorrow night there won't be a trace of this."

In the end Hannah had agreed with Paulie: his dad was a horn dog and his mother was weak.

But there were things Paulie admired about his father. His dad had saved more lives than Paulie could count. He had pulled bleeding or burned victims from the edge of death; he had even gone into a freezing river once to rescue a woman and her baby from the roof of a car. His pay was modest, the hours unpredictable, and failure at times inevitable. Paulie admired his dad's *toughness* but he'd vowed never to turn into that guy when it came to relationships.

But what Paulie did wasn't *like* that. It *wasn't*.

The idea of swimming without the wetsuit—in only his Speedo—tempts him. He knows the water is in the low fifties, testicle-numbing at best, but if you can take it for just a few minutes, the body actually feels warm. Stay in too long and you flirt with hypothermia, but he's done it before and it's pretty exhilarating as extreme sports go. He stuffs the wetsuit back in the car and walks toward the end of the dock, hyperventilating, determined, laughing inside when he considers he's providing his own punishment. Ten feet from the end he takes three long strides and dives.

• • •

Hannah walks into her bedroom after coming up empty scanning the guest room for possible missed clues, throws her car keys and cell on top of the dresser, and flops onto the bed. She wishes she had asked Mary more questions. Mr. Wells was weird today—if *she'd* gone missing, her parents wouldn't have been asking witnesses what they were doing out so late; they'd have been desperate and welcoming of any useful information. And what about *Mrs.* Wells?

She clicks the remote, looking for the evening news. A local talk show host pops on the screen so she hits the mute button, rolls over, and gathers her pillow. For those few quick moments this morning when she thought Mary Wells might be . . . well, dead—in the time between when she saw the news on TV and then the impossibility of that news registered—she also thought about Paulie. What if something happened to Paulie? Would this be how she wanted her last time with him to be? There was a moment of clarity that almost made her text him.

She rolls over to see Dr. Johannsen filling the flat screen, standing before a mike with a large 4 on it. Mr. Logs stands in the background. Hannah un-mutes.

". . . news of Ms. Wells's disappearance. It was kind of automatic," Dr. Johannsen is saying. "We got parental permission for the students we sent and it was the most natural thing to load a bus and see if we could assist. A teacher supervised and the police department directed the operation."

"Were there students present *without* parental permission?" Mallory Preston, local TV reporter, asks.

Dr. Johannsen looks at her askance. "Not that I know of," she says, and smiles. "I'll have a better idea about that tomorrow morning. The important thing is, those students are safe and the young woman in question, whatever her difficulty, seems not to have been the victim of foul play."

"Speaking of Ms. Wells," the reporter says, "do you have any further knowledge of her whereabouts?"

"I don't," Dr. Johannsen says. "I'm sure more will become apparent in the next few days."

"Have you had a conversation with her father since the search was called off?"

"No. We'll handle it through our attendance office like any other absence. This is a good student with an exemplary record, both academically and socially."

"I wonder—"

"What will happen," Dr. Johannsen interrupts, "is something newsworthy, and you folks will concentrate on that and we'll get on with the business of finishing up our school year. Thank you, but I have work to do."

Right on, Dr. Jo! Hannah thinks. *Slap that nosy bitch!* Hannah's cell has been ringing every ten minutes and she knows Mallory Preston and her colleagues want her on the record about her encounter with Mary, which is *not* going to happen. *Fifteen minutes of fame, my ass,* she thinks. *I'm saving mine for something fun.*

Paulie pulls himself onto the dock after nearly forty-five minutes in the icy reservoir. It was a good, fast workout and he feels on top of the world, warm and strong. *Warm* will give way to violent shivering in minutes when sensation returns and his body reacts to the astonishing cold. He slides his feet into his flip-flops, rushes to the car and pulls on his sweats, slips into the driver's seat, and cranks the heat to high while backing away from the dock. As he approaches the city limits, the shivering starts and a half-mile later he pulls over because he's paying way more attention to his vibrating body than to his driving. *If I died right now they'd set my time of death two hours ago based on body temperature.* He laughs at the thought and sits another twenty minutes with the car heater slowly bringing him back toward 98.6. When the intensity of the shivering has diminished enough to let him clutch the steering wheel with a degree of confidence, he drives home, strips out of his sweats, and lowers himself into a bath. He considers the events of the past few days, wondering if he should go ahead and tell all he knows.

"Bobby Wright!" Paulie says as The Rocket door *cushes* closed behind Bobby. He looks at his watch; ten fifteen. "Aren't you out past curfew?"

Bobby looks confused.

"I'm messing with you, man. What can I do for you? Still got coffee that's almost fresh. A day-old croissant?"

Bobby frowns again.

"Still messin' with you, buddy. What do you need?"

"Like a pop or something," Bobby says.

Paulie nods toward the cooler. "Pop we got. Coke, Pepsi, hell we even have Jolt and Red Bull in the back. Keep you hoppin' all night."

Bobby's eyes shift side to side. "Is that what you've been drinking?"

"Naw, man. I'm just bored. Got an hour and a half to go."

Paulie watches Bobby walk toward the cooler. The

kid moves like he's afraid he'll trip a landmine. He stands staring through the glass at the soda pop, unable to decide. He opens the cooler door, closes it again, opens it.

"No matter which one you pick, you're gonna wish you'd got the other one," Paulie says.

Bobby turns around. "Huh?"

"Messin' with you again. Grab one, it's on me."

"I can pay for it." Bobby reaches in his pocket, shows Paulie a five.

"Yeah, man, but you don't *have* to. I'm buyin'. All you gotta do is stay here to drink it."

"Really? You want me to stay here?"

Paulie looks at his watch again. "You got some place to go?"

"No . . . I mean, usually nobody . . . I can drink it here."

"All right then, grab what you want and pull up a chair." He nods toward a table near the counter.

Bobby grabs a Dr Pepper and moves to sit. "I can pay for it . . ." he says again.

"But you're not gonna," Paulie says. "Sit."

Bobby sits.

Paulie claps his hands together. "So what do you want to talk about?"

Bobby's eyes widen. Bobby Wright does not often

experience cool guys treating him like he's visible.

"C'mon," Paulie says, "what's up?"

Bobby takes a drink of his pop. "Actually . . ."

"Shoot."

"How'd you learn to swim like that? Like up at the lake an' stuff?"

Paulie walks around the counter, hoists himself up. "You know, swimming lessons when I was little. Then I joined the Parks and Rec swim team so I could get a coach. Cool thing about swimming is, if you keep doing it you get faster. Pretty soon I started wondering how far I could go. Found out Mr. Logs was a wannabe channel swimmer and just started doing it with *him*. Guy's a beast."

"You think I could learn?"

"Sure. Can you swim?"

"Yeah, I took those lessons."

"Just go down to one of the city pools when they open this summer. Tell 'em you want to join the novice team. Go from there. How come you want to swim?"

Bobby reddens, looks at the table. "I don't know. I guess it kind of seems cool."

Paulie gives a short laugh. "It's more than cool," he says. "It's colder than hell."

Bobby smiles. "I'll bet. You think you'd be different? You know, if you didn't swim."

"Yeah," Paulie says, "I'd be different."

"Like how?"

"I don't know. Swimming, like that's a challenge. First time you get in water that cold you can't fucking believe you're doing it. In fact, the first time you just get back out."

"How'd you get back in?"

"Logs called me a pussy."

"Mr. Logsdon called you that?"

"He didn't say the word," Paulie says, "but he said it. Then when you do finally get used to the water, it's still hard work."

Bobby's eyes dart around the room.

"You really thinking of trying it?"

Bobby grimaces.

"Hey, I thought the same thing," Paulie says, "but that shit makes you tough, and there's nothing wrong with that. Listen man, you sign up for summer swimming soon as school is out and get a few miles under your belt. Logs an' I'll take you out when you wanna give it a shot. The water will be warm by then. Meantime do some running. Lift some weights."

Bobby finishes his pop and stands. "I tried the weight room once," he says. "But all those big guys . . . Arney Stack was in there and some other guys. I just left."

"Naw man, fuck that. Those guys just make all the noise. Especially Stack. If you'd have stayed you'd have seen a whole bunch of regular guys."

Bobby moves toward the door. "Think you could go down there with me once? Like, show me how the machines work and stuff?"

"*Hell* yeah," Paulie says. "I go a couple times a week, on days I don't swim. Bring your gear day after tomorrow."

Bobby opens the door, hesitates. "Okay, then," he says. "Day after tomorrow. Weight room." He smiles and is gone.

The classroom is abuzz when Logs closes the door for the beginning of Period 8 the next day.

"Guess I already know 'what's up' today, huh?" he says.

"Did they find her?" someone asks.

"I haven't heard," he says.

"Something's messed up," Justin says. "Lotta time between when Mary was gone from home and when we went looking."

"You have to admit, Mr. Logs, something's strange," Marley Waits says.

"There *are* unanswered questions," Logs says. He takes a deep breath. "We need to be careful how we deal with this. Mary's one of us and I'm guessing she'll be here again soon. We have to be respectful now, and when she comes back."

"Yeah," Hannah says. "I'd be pretty embarrassed if my dad called out the troops when I wasn't really missing."

"Well," Logs says, "as I understand it, Mr. Wells rescinded his missing persons report."

"She'll be back," Arney says, "and this will all make sense. We should make it easy for her. None of us would want to be in her shoes." He shakes his head. "I don't get it about the torn-up room."

"Or the fact that nobody saw it but her parents," Marley says.

"How about instead of wild adolescent speculation," Logs says, "we talk about how we felt out there looking for her? It sure wasn't the way I wanted to wrap up my teaching career."

"I was just praying I wouldn't be the one to find her," Josh Takeuchi says. "I kept thinkin', *leaves and dirt in her face, eyes all glassed over, marks on her neck; please God don't let it be me."*

"You've been watching too many *Criminal Minds* reruns, Tak," Hannah says.

Josh opens another sandwich bag. "Maybe so," he replies, "but I'm telling you . . ."

"Luckily, it didn't have to be anyone," Logs says. "Actually that's a pretty sane reaction."

Hannah laughs. "I thought wrestlers are supposed to be tough."

"Exactly," Tak says, "and if I didn't want it to be me, I mean, I wanted *someone* to find her, if she was out there. Kind of cowardly to want her found but let her ghost haunt someone else."

"Cowardly, maybe," Logs says, "but I found *myself* looking under some piles of leaves with held breath and gritted teeth." He surveys the room. "Anyone else?"

Up goes Bobby Wright's hand.

Logs closes his eyes. "I'm not going to win this, am I, Bobby? You will raise your hand at my funeral."

Bobby pulls his hand down. "I just thought, what if it was over all of a sudden. You know, way too soon."

"Say more."

"We thought she was probably dead. At least I did. She was here one day and then just gone, like for no good reason. I just thought, what if that was me? I sit around thinking of all the stuff I'm gonna do someday, you know, when I get it together. What if there's no someday?"

No shit, Paulie thinks.

"So I'm out there in the woods, thinking, man, I *better* get it together, and I feel, like, ready to do that. Like I crank myself up. And then—and this is bad—they find out Mary isn't really missing and . . ." Bobby shakes his head. ". . . and I already feel it draining out. I know I'm not going to have the guts." He shakes his head. "I went home yesterday thinking, what a schmuck . . . somebody's gotta die for me to be brave."

I will get that little bugger into the weight room, Paulie thinks, *and then I will get him into the water.*

Logs walks over and sits on a table at the side of the room. In a low voice he says, "Wow."

Justin snorts, running a hand through his short hair. "Seems to me that was pretty brave right there."

Bobby looks off to the side.

"Don't do that," Justin says. "You feel like you feel

because you shrink off all the time. You look right in my eye and say, 'Damn right it was brave, Justin Chenier.'"

The trace of a smile crosses Bobby's lips again. He glances at Paulie, who nods.

"Fuckin' *say* it," Justin says.

Bobby looks at the ceiling.

"Don't make me get up."

"Damn right it was brave, Justin Chenier."

"A'ight then," Justin says and turns to Logs. "So, Brother Logs, when we get to hear the *climax* to this saga?'"

"Soon as there is one, I suspect," Logs says.

"Whatever's going on with Mary," Arney says, "she's not going to let a shot at another four-point-plus GPA and more than a hundred thousand in scholarship money go down the drain. Trust me, she'll come around."

Paulie has been taking it all in. He frowns. *Ol' Arney. Always in the know. Even when he isn't.*

"And I'm guessing I can get her to bring us up to speed," Arney says. "I've spent some time with her." He looks at Bobby. "She's more willing to talk about the important stuff than you might think."

Justin sits up. "You mean . . ."

"Get your head out of the gutter," Arney says. "I just

mean she's not as *surface* as everyone thinks. She's just careful."

"Mr. Logs," Paulie says, "If you were sitting in a bar having a beer with your best friend with none of us around, what would you be saying you think happened?"

"You think I drink beer?"

"C'mon, man."

"I don't know what I'd say, but I get your point, Paulie. This is Period 8, where we let it all hang out. I'm being careful because when we don't understand something, it's because we don't have enough information. Let's keep focused on how you were feeling."

"Long as we're baring our souls . . ." Heads turn toward Taylor Max. *Baring our souls* comes out sarcastically. She pushes her dark bangs away from her eyes. "I think she was lucky."

Silence.

Logs says, "Why lucky?"

Taylor hesitates, testing the waters with her eyes. Taylor Max would be pretty, if her life weren't all over her face— and she's tough as nails. Taylor isn't silent because she's shy. Taylor is silent because she doesn't believe anyone wants to hear what she has to say.

"I come here, to this class, to learn something—anything—that goes against what I think the world is like," she says. "But I always go away thinking I've got it about right."

She takes in the room again, and says, under her breath, "What the hell.

"I've heard the same stuff everyone else hears," she says. "Mary's dad is a control freak, makes her give him her cell phone every day so he can look at the call history, calls the numbers he doesn't recognize. He made her sign the 'Saving Myself for Marriage' vow, or whatever they call it. He's not even religious, just has to have control. Who knows what's true? The only times I've ever seen him, he looked like any parent, kind of quiet, maybe a little stern."

Taylor breathes deep. "But I caught her crying in the bathroom once last year. She was, like, *way* not Mary. So I said right out what I thought. She didn't deny any of it. If somebody says your dad's a beast and he's not, you deny it."

Taylor scans the room; doesn't catch any looks of disagreement. She shakes her head. "That shit is poison."

Silence.

She shrugs. "My mom's been bringing control freaks into me and my brother's lives for fucking ever, excuse my shitty language. They're all the same. Look good at first, start to take over and try to convince you the crap they want you to do is for your own good. I don't know how it works in Mary Wells's house, but the more they get burrowed in the more power they get. If you've got a mom like ours, she's so glad to have a man around the house she'll believe anything. Pretty soon she's just the gravy train for a pig. Good thing about my mother is, she finally recognizes it and gets rid of the bastard. Like I said, I don't know what Mary Wells's mom is like, but I see Mr. Wells and I get a feeling in my gut that is *way* familiar. And if you'd have seen her in the bathroom that day, you wouldn't start asking me a bunch of dumb questions or telling me why my situation is different."

Nobody is about to do that.

"And by the way," Taylor adds, "after she gets rid of the bastard? She goes and gets another one. But that's a story for another time." She puts her head down on her arms. "Anyway, that's why I thought she was lucky. Any escape is an escape. She was out."

"I'm with Taylor," Hannah says. "Anybody who has that much control over his kid is creepy. And I'd say that if Mary were in the room."

Arney Stack stands. "Maybe you guys are right," he

says. "Maybe I do have it wrong, and this is going to sound like some geeky ASB president . . ."

Justin says, "Tell us somethin' we don't know."

"We have to do something about this," Arney says. "I don't mean just about Mary, but all of it. There's not much a student body officer can do in a school, it's not like we influence educational policy or anything. But we ought to at least figure out how to have each other's backs."

Paulie glances at Justin.

"A lot of us have been in school together four years, some even longer than that. No offense, Bobby, but if your family wasn't in the paper for receiving Christmas charity I wouldn't even know who you are."

Bobby looks stricken. His family's picture on the front of the Regional section of the local newspaper is the embarrassment of his high school career.

Arney catches Bobby's look. "I didn't mean . . . Hey, man, I just meant we don't have each other's backs like we should."

Justin puts his head down.

"Look, we're in this together. I get to be student body president because no matter how much I pump iron, I lack the skills to be what I really want to be, which is a super-jock. So I teach myself to speak in public and do the political thing. Hell, Bobby, you're every bit as smart as I am and twice as sensitive, given what you just told us, but somebody's been pushing you around making you think all you can do is survive. Man, go check it out with your parents . . . okay, not *your* parents, but some adult, maybe Mr. Logs, and get him to tell you how many of the cool guys and girls in high school turned out to be duds once they got out in the real world. My dad makes over a half-million a year in one of the most prestigious law firms in this town and he was voted 'Kid Most Likely to Get Beat Up By Someone from a Lower Grade' in high school. I just meant . . ."

"It's okay," Bobby says. "I know you didn't mean anything."

"My point is," Arney continues, "that one thing the whole student body can do is start recognizing who we all are. I'm ticked off at myself because I've been judging the people who come in here every day and don't say anything. I mean, if I hadn't started getting to know Mary . . . well, I'm just saying we need some kind of decency campaign in this school. *That's* what I'm going to shoot for the rest of my time."

Paulie thinks, *Arney just fucked Bobby and got Bobby to let him off the hook. Business as usual.*

The bell rings and no one moves. Arney picks up his books as if nothing has happened. Gradually everyone else begins packing up and heading out.

"Hey, Mr. Logs," Paulie says at the door, "can I talk with you a minute?"

Logs slaps his forehead. "That's right, you *said* you needed to talk with me. Sorry." He closes the door behind Hannah, who just walked by as if Paulie didn't exist.

"Ready for TMI?"

Logs frowns.

"She's the one."

"The one . . ."

"Mary Wells. She's who I cheated on Hannah with."

.7

"Hannah was at that debate tournament," Paulie says.

"I'm not sure I want to hear this. You sure you want to tell it?"

"I didn't, but that was before all this craziness."

Logs says, "What the hell, this is my last year."

"So Arney wants me to go over to the Armory and listen to Justin and his new group, and a couple of other groups he's tight with. I'm already planning to go so I say I'll meet him.

"We're early and they've got a bunch of pretenders for the first hour or so, guys whose parents should *never* have given them music lessons, and we're shootin' the shit, waiting for Justin and his guys. I look over at this girl who I catch looking at me and I barely recognize her. I mean, she looks like Mary except she has this *way* low-cut sweater."

Logs frowns, in disbelief rather than disapproval.

"Swear to god, man, I'm not out looking. I'm not."

"I believe you."

"Pretty soon she's beside me. She says hi to Arney and we're watching and she's bumping me, like almost by accident. But then we're talking, almost yelling over the music, 'cause Jus is on now and he's cranking it up, and her hand is on my arm and they start to play a slow one and she asks me to dance. I don't want to, but it's Mary Wells. Even if Hannah's friends see me, it's the Virgin Mary. I could get in as much trouble dancing with Arney."

"Why do I think you should have danced with Arney?"

"No kidding. Anyway she leans into me, arms around my neck, pressed up against me. This is not the Mary Wells I have come to know and yell 'Go Team Go' at. The second it starts feeling good, I start feeling bad and I push her away. She backs off a little and we finish the dance and I'm looking around the room and a couple of Hannah's friends *are* watching so I know I need to get my ass home.

"I tell Arney I've gotta cut it short, go up to the stage

and tell Justin he rocks, and head for the parking lot. Only when I get to my car, there's Mary goddamn Wells."

Logs frowns, again in disbelief, though he knows the one guy he always believes is Paulie Bomb.

"She wants a ride home. I ask who she came with and she says, 'Julie Fricke and some other cheerleaders, but they left,' and something feels wrong, because the cheerleaders stick together. They're jocks."

"So . . . you took her home?"

"Kind of. I stall for a while, then I see Arney coming out of the Armory and I holler at him. He drives over, rolls down the window, and I tell him to give Mary a ride; she lives on his way. He says no-can-do, he'd really like to but he's headed to some midnight thing with the YFC kids. Are you kidding me? Arney Stack doing midnight come-to-Jesus with Youth for Christ? I mentioned this but he says he'd promised to help them get Johannsen to let them hold meetings in a classroom as long as it was after school. I said, 'Arney, you won the election. You can't run again, this is high school. Campaign promises aren't even real promises in high school!' but he said something about being a politician with a new kind of ethics, to which I said a *new kind* would be *some*."

"It's too late to make a long story short, but give it a try, 'cause you are killing me."

"I'm driving toward her house and she says, 'Could we just drive around for a while?' and I say huh-uh because 'I'm promised.'"

"You said you were *promised*?"

"When in doubt, go with comedy," Paulie says. "So she says, 'I just don't want to go home yet. My dad . . .' and she lets it trail off, and I'm pissed at my dad half the time—and *really* mad at him the other half—so I said maybe we could drive around a little, but not too long. This felt bad, and I wasn't even *doing* anything."

"Yet," Logs says.

"So we drove out past Diamond Lake and then along High Drive and through a couple of neighborhoods and I said I *had* to take her home. We got within a few hundred yards of that long-ass driveway that goes up to her mansion and she told me to stop. I'm goin' *no way* but she showed me her watch and said I did *not* want to be the guy caught driving up her driveway this close to midnight. I thought, most rumors are rumors for a reason and maybe the one about her dad being a teenage boy killer is one of them. So I stopped."

Logs closes his eyes.

"I told her I'd wait until she got at least to the driveway. She wanted a few minutes to 'collect' herself, like she was really worried about her old man. Then she started asking me stuff like why I thought she couldn't get a steady boyfriend. She was calm, like she really wanted to know, so I said the dumb-ass thing: I said well, she didn't always look quite as hot as she looked right then, and she asked if I thought she was pretty, and I said sure, everyone thought she was pretty. She asked if I thought she was hot, and I was trying to think of a way to say she was without saying she was hot to *me*. But I gotta tell you Logs, my mind was wandering to a bad place."

"At this point your mentor would rather hear generalizations," Logs says.

Paulie snorts. "Before I could say anything she put her arms around my neck and asked if I wanted . . . if I wanted . . ."

"To have sex?"

"Yeah, but she said the *word*."

This is so far out of Logs's experience of Mary Wells he can barely believe it, even coming from Paulie.

"I don't know if you know what that *does* . . ."

"I know what it does," Logs says.

"Believe it or not, I was still thinking of Hannah," Paulie says. "I pushed Mary away, but she was like, desperate. It was like some kind of test of life or death or something. This probably sounds like a guy making excuses for doing something spectacularly dumb, but it's the truth. I pushed her away and she started crying, sobbing almost. This is crazy but did you ever have sex with someone because you felt *sorry* for them? That's not *human*, is it? I mean, I can't say I didn't get cranked up; *that's* not human either, but then she was rubbing me and her shirt was off and she was like an *animal*. When it was over I just wanted her out of my car, because *sanity* comes rushing back with . . . well, you know what I'm saying. But she wouldn't get out. She wanted to know if she was *good*."

Logs simply shakes his head.

"She straightened herself up and asked again if she was good, I mean, like a little kid wanting to know if she tied her shoes right. I said yeah just to get her out of there, then I watched her walk down the road and turn into her driveway, and sat there another five minutes wanting to beat my head against the dashboard 'til I went unconscious."

"That would have been the smartest thing you did all night."

"By the time I'd driven two miles, I knew I'd have to tell Hannah. I read Shakespeare; I know about tangled webs. So I did, the very next day, and that was that. So when all of a sudden Mary was missing and then she wasn't, and the more we heard the stranger it got, I started thinking something's *way* out of whack here. I did what I did and it's my fault, but Mary was a whole different girl than the one everyone calls Jesus's mom. I paid attention in psych. That kind of behavior means secrets."

"What are you thinking?"

"Messed-up room that nobody saw, two-day lag in reporting . . ."

"What I said in P-8 today goes double for your brain, Paulie," Logs says. "You know what they say about assuming."

"That it makes an ass out of 'u' and me?"

"No, that it makes whoever does it an asshole. So sit tight. I've said it before, and I'll say it again—most of the time when we don't understand it's because we don't know enough. We need to know more."

• • •

Only minutes before midnight, Logs unlocks the double doors to the pool at the university and lets himself in, grateful that Coach Graves entrusted him with a key years ago. "If you drown in there," the coach had said with a smile, "I'll tell them you lifted the keys from my jacket."

Logs doesn't turn on the overhead lights, knowing the glow from the exit signs and the maintenance room will cast enough light to see the end lines and the wall. He and Paulie are connected by water; both go there for solace and both go there to think. He stands on the starting block, breathes deep, and shoots out over the middle lane.

Paulie's right. Something is *off*. He settles into a pace he could hold all night. Even at this age, Bruce Logsdon swims like most people walk. He could almost do this in the dark. He knows in his gut the number of strokes from one end to the other at any level of fatigue. The water is like a womb. It is safe.

As he flips in and out of his turns, he considers what he heard in Period 8 today. He's always known there were stories, but hasn't always known which ones belong to which student. He's always surprised to see where rugged stuff lands.

I wouldn't even know your name. Arney's words to Bobby

Wright. Absent the mindless shot Arney took at Bobby's poverty, they could have been Logs's words, or almost any other kid's in the room. So many times the greatest pain slides in under the radar. He doesn't judge himself by what he's missed, but he's aware it's a lot. Probably this Mary Wells thing will blow over; a feasible explanation will reveal itself and time will pass. P-8 has yielded some unexpected intimacies over the years, but there was a *feeling* in that room today. For a brief moment, mortality raised its head among these kids, and it mined stories from a deeper lode.

While Logs cranks out laps over at the university pool, Paulie swamps out The Rocket restrooms, watching the wide-angle mirror for late-night university students pulling all-nighters or the occasional homeless person stepping in to get out of the cold, and feeling the fatigue brought on by a day that started with an early morning swim and is ending with a late-night shift. He is blessed with the part of his father's DNA he welcomes—the ability to operate at pretty much full capacity on five hours' sleep—but the stress of this day is taking its toll. He rolls the mop bucket and cleaning tools toward the back room, preparing to close out the till and lock up for the night, when the bell over the door jingles.

"Paulie Bomb."

"Hey, Arney, what's goin' on?"

"Had a business meeting with some guys. I'm just headed home."

"A *business* meeting. What kind of business meeting happens at midnight? And what high school kid has a business meeting *any* time? Man, Stack, you are a different kind of dude."

"Ah, my old man wants me to learn about investing. Gave me some capital and the guys I'm working with had to meet late. Couldn't fit my school schedule into their business day."

"Must have been *some* capital," Paulie says.

"If everything works out," Arney says, "they'll get a good return. Me, too."

"I'm closing up," Paulie says. "Got coffee in the thermoses, but nothing fresh."

"No coffee," Arney says back. "I thought you'd probably be here. Wanted to ask you something."

Paulie stacks the bills in the lock box and opens the overnight safe. "Have to be *real* quick," he says. "I'm beat."

"What would you think if I started hanging out with Hannah?"

The bottom drops out of Paulie's gut. He doesn't answer.

Arney says, "You guys are done, right?"

"Hannah is."

"I know it'd feel kind of funny, but we almost had something going when we were sophomores, back before you guys were—"

"It wouldn't feel funny, Arney," Paulie says. His eyes go cold. "It would feel shitty." He picks up a thermos and walks it to the sink, removing the lid and dumping the last of the coffee. "But if you want to go out with Hannah and Hannah wants to go out with you, there's nothing I can do about it." He puts the thermos in the sink, runs hot water into it. "There's nothing I *should* do about it."

"I just don't want—"

"Do whatever," Paulie says. "I made this bed and I'm sleeping in it whether I like it or not."

"I couldn't let it to get in the way of our friendship."

"Look, Arney, I'm not gonna be a dick and get in the way if it's something real. If I did, *that* would affect our friendship." Paulie's doubting the friendship as he says it.

"This is just a little quick, is all. Feels like revenge."

Arney purses his lips.

"Not by you. Hannah."

"Look man, if you'd rather—"

Paulie throws up his hands, palms out. "Naw, man, do it. If I'm going to purge this shit, I best purge it all at once."

"Okay, but only if you're sure."

"I'm sure!" He watches Arney walk toward the door, and slams the safe shut.

"Want me to kick his ass for you?" Justin leans against Paulie's Beetle the next day, moments after last bell, watching the building empty.

Paulie laughs. "I could do that myself."

"But there's a certain pleasure to hiring it done," Justin says. "Man, that is *cold*. There's *got* to be a code." Justin is not a big guy; five-nine, a hundred-fifty pounds, with five percent body fat and the strength of guys half again his size. He'd give Arney a run.

"He just asked if it was okay. You know Arney, always testing shit. If Hannah's interested, well, that tells me something about Hannah." He reaches for the door handle. "Suck-it-up time for me either way. If it's not

Stack, it'll be someone else eventually. I can't shut down the head movies no matter who it is. Hannah's pissed and she's pretty good at 'letting you know how it feels.' Got a feeling I'll be logging some *miles*. On the court and on the sea."

"I thought you guys were friends," Hannah says, sitting in Arney's Audi in the Taco Time parking lot, her back against the passenger-side door.

"We are friends," Arney says. "But I don't have a lot of respect for what he did. I hate that stuff. Besides, Paulie's okay with it. He said you guys are history."

"*That* was easy," Hannah says.

"I thought the same thing. But he said you were clear it was over, too."

Hannah says, "I will *not* be treated like that."

"Well, you won't have to worry about it with me."

Hannah glares. "Arney, we're talking about hanging out, not getting together."

Arney backs up. "I know, I know. I just meant—"

"It will be a long time before I do that again. I sure as *hell* don't need a boyfriend to make me whole."

"I was just saying . . . I'm just not like that, is all."

"Well, it might give Paulie a chance to think about what he messed up."

"Yeah, there's that." Arney smiles.

"I need to think about it." She looks across the parking lot at a minivan full of teenagers pulling in. "You can buy me a burrito. Prove your intentions."

Justin Chenier gets out of the backseat of the minivan and squints, watching Arney and Hannah disappear into Taco Time. While the rest of his friends head for the entrance, he crosses the street to Arby's.

.8

Arney Stack walks toward the exit at Comstock Savings and Loan with Woody Hansen, a well-dressed man in his late twenties.

"You're doing a great job," Woody says. "You have unusual instincts for a person your age."

"Thanks, Woody," Arney says dismissively. "'Preciate it." He slings his backpack over his shoulder and hurries toward the door.

Woody steps out onto the sidewalk with him. "You know the risks here, right?"

"Yeah," Arney says. "I know the risks."

"It's been smooth sailing so far, thanks mostly to you, but if things go south, there's no backing out."

"Do you know my dad?" Arney asks.

"Mostly by reputation," Woody says.

"Well, if you know him, you know what my resolve is like. I won't be backing out," Arney says. "I was born for this. Man, I can hardly wait to get out of high school and into the real world full time. The old man wants me to be a businessman. I'll give it to him in spades."

Woody slaps him on the back. "You're an unusual man, Master Stack," he says, smiling.

"Rubbing shoulders with the mucky-mucks, huh?" Hannah says as Arney gets in the car.

"Not really," he says. "Guy's kind of a dick. My dad gave me some money to invest; he wants me to know how to handle finances. Like, *real* finances. This guy—he's like third in command at this place—got me in with a couple of lawyers, plus the guy who runs Mountain Sports and the Quality Comfort Motel. We've thrown in on some investments."

"Wow. You're like an *adult*." Hannah laughs.

"Kinda," Arney says. "Dad gave me a big enough grubstake that they at least have to *treat* me like one."

"Never hurts to have a little leverage, I guess."

Arney nods. "So," he says. "Wanna see a movie tonight?"

Hannah hesitates, then, "Sure, why not?"

"You cool with it? Paulie and all?"

"I said yes. That means I'm cool with it. Don't keep asking me that, Arney. If we want to see a movie, we see a movie."

"How 'bout I pick you up about seven thirty?"

"Great." It doesn't really feel great, but every time she thinks about Paulie, of what he did, a fire smolders deep inside.

Two hours later Arney sits across the table from Mary Wells at Marv's, a small pizza joint on the outskirts of town. "You sure everything's okay? I was worried about you."

"I'm sure," she says. "Things just got crazy."

"I was worried you were going to blow it all," Arney says, reaching across the table and grabbing her wrist. "You know what would have happened if you hadn't shown back up, like with your future and all?"

"It's all I hear, Arney."

"It put your parents in a real spot." He runs his hand

lightly across the top of hers, still holding her wrist with the other.

"Look, I'm sorry," Mary says. "I am. I'm getting it back together. Things are fine with Dad." She tries to pull her hand away. Arney holds it gently but firmly, runs the back of his finger down the side of her cheek. "Okay," he says. "I was worried, that's all. You have so much to lose."

Logs and Paulie hoist themselves onto the dock at the end of a three-mile swim, both gasping for air.

"Man," Paulie says, "you gotta quit trying to shame me in those last five hundred yards. You *know* I'm not going to let you win."

"I win every time I pull myself out of the water," Logs says. "Before long I won't even be able to challenge you. I gotta feel dangerous as long as I can."

"You'll die dangerous," Paulie says. He looks past the other end of the dock at a luxury car parked next to his Beetle. He elbows Logs. "Who's that?"

Logs squints to focus, shakes his head. "Sucks getting old," he says. "I gotta get closer."

Mary Wells leans out the driver's side window as they approach her father's Lexus. "Hey."

Logs stops. "Mary Wells."

"Mary Wells," Paulie says right behind him.

She looks down sheepishly, recovers. "I thought I'd find you here, Mr. Logsdon. I just wanted to apologize for missing Period 8 the last few days."

"No apology necessary. It's completely voluntary."

"I know, but I've been there every day since the middle of my freshman year; I thought I owed you an explanation."

"You don't owe it, but I'd love to hear one. You've kind of singlehandedly turned the school on its head this past week."

"I know. I have a lot of apologizing to do. And a bunch of work to make up. I just wanted you to know I'm okay."

He looks at the car. "I take it you've seen your dad."

Mary nods.

"Good," Logs says. "I was starting to worry about your scholarship."

"Me, too." She raises her eyebrows. "Could I talk with you for a minute, Paulie?"

Paulie studies her.

"That's my clue," Logs says. "Got to get home to my cat. He gets all surly when I'm late."

Paulie turns for his car.

"Please," Mary says.

Paulie stops. What the hell. "I gotta get my sweats."

"I'll wait."

Paulie sits in the passenger seat of the Beetle after removing the wetsuit, a towel covering his legs and butt while he struggles out of his swimsuit and pulls on a pair of sweat pants. *I should drive the fuck out of here.* But seconds later he's standing next to the Lexus.

"I'm sorry," she says.

Paulie gazes at her without expression. He didn't realize how angry he was until he saw her sitting there. When she was maybe dead and then missing he felt the same compassion and confusion everyone else felt, but she's here and all put together again, and he aches for what he lost.

"I know you and Hannah split," she says. "It was my fault."

Paulie looks over the glossy black roof at the reservoir. He can't trust himself to talk.

"I'll make it up to you, Paulie. I will."

"How are you going to do that? How are you going to do that, Mary? Jesus, what were you doing? I couldn't get away from you."

"I know," she says. "I was . . ." Tears stream down her cheeks. "I just don't want you to hate me. I couldn't stand that."

If anything will douse a fire raging inside Paulie Bomb, it's that. "Look," he says, pushing his wet hair off his forehead. "I don't get it, but I can't blame *you*. I'm the guy in charge of my zipper."

"If I went to Hannah . . ."

"Jesus."

"I could tell her . . ."

"She'd kick your ass. And nothing would change between her and me, unless it got worse."

"*Worse?*"

"Worse. You're the Virgin Mary for chrissake. She'd think I . . ."

"She's not *stupid*."

Paulie takes a long breath. "Mary, there can't be another guy who's ever seen you like that. I'll bet half the guys at the Armory thought it was you but knew it couldn't be. Hell, I could walk into any boys' locker room at Heller and tell them what happened and they'd laugh me out. C'mon, you know . . ."

"Do you have any idea what it's like—"

Paulie slaps his open hand hard against the roof of the car, and Mary flinches. He breathes deep, pushing back equal parts of rage and pity, and curiosity. "Sorry. Tell me what it's like."

"You don't want to know."

"Tell me."

"God, you hate me."

He closes his eyes. "Look, Mary, you said you wanted to talk to me. I'm listening. I don't hate you. I'm pissed but I'm as pissed at myself as I am at you. More pissed. If telling me what it's like to be you helps me get it, then tell me what it's fucking like."

She touches her forehead to the steering wheel. "It's like I can't just be me, *ever*, like there's this *thing* I'm supposed to be and I have to be it. No matter how bad I feel or how much I hate how everyone sees me, there's nothing I can do to change it. It's like a black hole, it sucks you in and there's not even a trace of you." She closes her eyes. "When your life is like that, you do things . . . things you don't understand. This is stupid," she says. "You don't want to know this." She stares out the windshield, quiet. Then, almost as if to someone else, "There are spies everywhere."

"What?"

Mary doesn't seem to hear.

"Spies?" Paulie says. "What are you talking about?"

Mary's head jerks. She hesitates, as if Paulie snapped her out of a daydream. "My dad," she says finally. "He knows things about me there's no *way* he could guess."

"Like . . ."

"One of his friends saw me at Taco Time, what was I doing there? Or somebody saw me driving up by the lake, wasn't I supposed to be home? There are forty thousand people in this town; there *can't* be that many coincidences. Half the time he knows what route I take from school for my Running Start classes and I take a different one every time, just to mess him up."

"So how did you get away being at the Armory that night? Or with disappearing? What about your mom?"

Mary looks out the side window. "My mother barely *exists*," she says. "She just does what my dad says."

Paulie knows a thing or two about irrational parent behavior. He watches Mary and shakes his head.

"All I ever hear from my mother is that my dad loves me and I should 'do his bidding.' I got to the Armory by telling him I had extra cheerleading practice. When I disappeared he was so freaked out he didn't know what to do."

"So getting with me was one of those things you barely understand?" His voice is tinged with skepticism.

"That's part of it."

"Why *me*?"

"You're safe. You don't hurt people."

Paulie sits back. *Great. I don't hurt people, so I get screwed.*

"I messed up. There's more to tell, but . . ."

"Jesus, don't stop now."

Mary leans back, grips the wheel until her knuckles are white. "Some awful things, Paulie. *Awful* things."

"Tell me."

"It wouldn't do you any good to know."

In a low, measured voice, he says, "Mary, it might do *you* some good for me to know, or at least for somebody to know." Paulie is being the Paulie who drives himself nuts. *Why can't I just say, "Tell it to your shrink"? I'm not supposed to be the fucking shrink. Why can't I still be that guy Justin thinks can have any girl he wants?*

She shakes her head. "Trust me."

If you want to talk, say it all or go fuck yourself. He's *that close* to saying it.

She sees it in his eyes. "That can't sound right coming from me," she says.

"Won't argue with that. You gotta admit, Mary. This is bizarre. Getting all up in my stuff, then running into Hannah in the middle of the road at midnight and then the whole school's looking for you dead in the woods. Hannah told Justin you were wigged *way* out when she found you. What was *that* about? And where did you go?"

"I told you, Paulie, I can't talk about it. It's taken care of now, though, so you don't have to worry."

"Were you high?"

"Paulie, come on."

"Hannah also told Justin you didn't even know where you were."

"Look, I was scared, okay? Can we leave it at that?"

"Not if I ran the zoo," Paulie says. "But I fucking don't run the zoo."

There's no open gym tonight, so Paulie drives aimlessly through neighborhoods killing time before putting in a couple of late hours cleaning up at The Rocket. He runs his earlier conversation with Mary over and over in his head and it still leaves him uneasy. *Awful things, Paulie.* What the fuck; he should get a million miles away from this.

The calories he's burned in the water today are catching

up with him and a giant bag of buttered popcorn fills his imagination, so he pulls into the parking lot shared by the mall and the 16-screen cineplex.

"Hey, Marley," he says to Marley Waits through the glass at the ticket booth.

"Hey, Paulie. Going to the movies alone, huh?"

Paulie smiles. "It's not that bad, yet," he says.

Marley looks at him with a hint of pity.

"What I need more than sympathy right now is popcorn," he says, grimacing. "Any chance you can get me in as far as the concession stand?" He raises his eyebrows.

Marley looks behind her to see that no bosses are near, then back at him, shaking her head. "Don't look at me like that," she says, "you're in enough trouble. And don't sneak in on me, okay?"

Paulie raises his right hand. "Good as my word," he says, and Marley flinches. "I had that coming. I promise I will go only as far as the popcorn stand."

"Listen," she says. "I'm really sorry about you and Hannah. I mean, I'm on her side and everything, but . . . well, I'm sorry."

Paulie turns to look behind him, aware he might be

holding up the line. There is none. "Hell, *I'm* on her side," he says, turning back. "It was dumb."

Marley shakes her head. "Who in the world did you . . ."

"Privileged," Paulie says.

"Have you seen Hannah's Facebook page?" Marley grimaces. "Man, I wouldn't want to be whoever the chick was if she finds out. I mean, have you seen the arms on her?"

Paulie smiles again. "I have seen the arms on her," he says. *I've also seen what they're attached to.* "Any chance I could get that popcorn?"

"Sure." Something behind him catches her eye and her face pales. "Don't look now. . . ."

But he does, in time to see Hannah getting out of the passenger side of Arney Stack's Audi. Arney walks around the car toward her, places a hand in the middle of her back as they walk toward the theater.

"Guess I wasn't as hungry as I thought," Paulie says. "Thanks anyway."

"Aw, Paulie." But he's gone. He jogs to his Beetle and in seconds is pulling onto the main street.

.9

When Mary Wells walks into Period 8 the following day, the room goes quiet.

"Ms. Wells," Logs says. "Welcome back."

"Thanks," she says in a near whisper, and moves sheepishly to a desk. She sits, hands folded on the flat surface in front of her.

"Don't mean to be pushy," Justin says, "but how about bringin' us up to speed."

Logs says, "Justin . . ."

"No," Mary says. "He's right." She's quiet again, glancing quickly at Hannah, then Paulie. Almost imperceptibly Paulie shakes his head, *don't do it*.

She looks at Arney, who smiles and nods.

"It was just some stuff at home," she says. "My dad . . . I got all worried about my scholarship and was thinking about taking a year at the university here. It got ugly and I took off. I don't know what my dad was doing reporting me missing like that." She puts her head down. "I'm so embarrassed."

Only the two or three students sitting adjacent to Hannah hear her singsongy whisper, "Buuullll-shit."

"That's it?" Justin says. Mary nods. "That's it. I was being stupid."

Logs watches. He starts to ask about her torn-up room, but lets it go. "It would be insincere not to acknowledge that we were talking about you," he says. "Or at least that we were talking about our responses to your disappearance."

Mary smiles. "It would be insincere to say I didn't know that."

"Any problem for you if we continue with our discussion?"

"No."

"Then, where were we?" Logs says.

Bobby Wright raises his hand. "Taylor was talking about bad guys."

Justin's head snaps up. "Bobby, my *man*," he says. "That's what I mean. Front and *center*."

"There's not much more to say," Taylor says, shifting in her seat. "I went home sick yesterday after this class. I hate even talking about that crap."

"You want to stop?" Logs asks.

Taylor looks at her desk. "I'm okay."

"What about your mom?" Hannah asks softly. "Guys like that have to have a way *in*."

"That's my mom," Taylor says. "A way in."

"No offense," Hannah says, "but file that under 'Why Some Women Need Two Assholes.'"

Paulie says, "Sweet, Hannah."

Hannah stares ahead as if she didn't hear.

"Who cares?" Taylor says. "The day I'm eighteen I'm out of there, even if I have to live in a cardboard box."

"If it comes to that, give me a call," Hannah says.

Justin says, "You got a cardboard box?"

Hannah doubles her fist and Justin raises his hands in surrender.

"Why is everything a joke to you, Justin?"

"Because everything is a joke," Justin says. "Sometimes it's a serious joke, but it's a joke just the same."

"That's just stupid."

"Some jokes are," Justin says, and turns sideways in

his chair to face Hannah. "We're sittin' in this nice safe room trying to figure out why Taylor's momma picks shitheads for boyfriends, or why Mary disappears and won't tell us why *really*, or whether guys are assholes for having brains in our di . . . not in our heads. Everybody acts like they don't know what bull it is when Arney goes Oprah on us at the same time he's messin' with Bobby, so we go ahead and pretend like we believe he's gonna lead us to having each other's backs." He looks at Arney and rolls his eyes.

"Look, I apologized," Arney says. "And I don't need *you* to believe me in order to do what's right."

"Good," Justin says back, "because I don't. We been buds a long time, Arney, but that doesn't mean I buy your stuff." He turns back to Hannah. "So that's why everything's a joke to me, Hannah Murphy."

A muffled sob comes from the back of the room and all eyes fall on Kylie Clinton, face against a desktop, body shaking. A hush falls over P-8 and Logs raises a hand. "This might be a good day to cut it short," he says. "Why don't we call it quits and you can all take a little break and be on time to your next class for the first time this year."

Mary gets up slowly, eyes locked on Kylie.

Arney touches Mary's elbow, nods toward the exit, pushes her gently in that direction.

The rest of the students gather their things and file silently out.

Paulie gives Logs a quick *see you at the lake*, throws his backpack over one shoulder, and heads to AP English.

Logs says softly to Bobby, who lingers at the door, "Would you hang out here in the hall for a while and tell my next class to wait if any of them shows early? I'll write you an excuse."

With the door closed and guarded, Logs sits in the chair next to Kylie. No acknowledgment, and the sobs continue. "Do you want to talk about it?" he says.

Head buried in her arms, she shakes it no.

"Would you like to see a counselor?"

The head shake is more emphatic.

Kylie's an unknown to Logs, pretty, quiet, new to Heller this year.

"Make you a deal. I'll take my next class across the hall; Ms. Kaywood's got prep. You stay here as long as you want and I'll cover for you with whatever your next class is, okay?"

"Fancher," Kylie says into the desk.

"No sweat. He owes me. But you have to talk to me

before you go home today, okay? Or at least to one of the counselors."

"You," Kylie says.

"Promise?"

She nods.

Logs gathers material for his next class and moves quietly out of the room, thanking Bobby for standing guard on his way across the hall.

Logs stands in Ms. Kaywood's classroom, watching Kylie Clinton through the window. She's sitting in his classroom staring straight ahead. A light rap on the door. He walks over and opens it.

"What's up, Arney?"

"You mind if I have a quick word with Kylie? I know her, I might be able to help."

Logs breathes deep. He knows from experience that a lot gets solved when the kids get involved, but he wasn't in total disagreement with what Justin said to Arney earlier. "Okay," he says. "But if she doesn't feel like talking, apologize, turn around, and leave."

"Aye, aye, sir," Arney says.

Logs watches as Arney enters the room, approaches Kylie

slowly. Kylie looks up, then away. Arney walks closer and puts a hand in the middle of Kylie's back, kneels, and talks. Kylie nods, nods again. Arney pats her on the shoulder and stands to leave and Kylie puts her head back down on the desk. Arney gives Logs a thumbs-up through the window and walks out.

When he returns to his classroom for the next period, Kylie is gone, but there's a note on the desk. *Thanks, Mr. Logs. I'm okay. I'll catch up with you today or see you in the morning. Thanks, really.*

Paulie walks into Frank's Diner and sits at the counter. In his opinion, Frank's serves the best hamburger in town and they make shakes the old-fashioned way; hard ice cream and they give you the container once they pour the glass full. No whipped cream on top and no sprinkles. Just good old vanilla ice cream and Hershey's chocolate syrup. Topped off with a side of onion rings, there are few greater delights from his limited culinary point of view.

It's not a popular hangout for kids, which is why he's here, desiring to sit with his thoughts, gorge, and try to forget Hannah.

Naomi Washburn is working the counter this evening. Naomi's a friend of his mother's. She started working at

Frank's three weeks after she dropped out of high school in the middle of her junior year and three husbands and five kids later makes a killer living on tips alone.

"Paulie Bomb," she says, ready to take his order. She squints, looking closer. "Honey, I've seen you looking worse but I can't for the life of me remember when."

"Hey, Naomi."

"What's going on, baby? You look shot at and missed, and shit at and hit."

"Tired," he says. "Been working out pretty hard."

"Your momma tells me that happens when the world's collapsing."

"Yeah, well, my momma's not exactly Dr. Phil. But I'll tell you, Naomi, I'm startin' to think I'm crazy."

"All you kids are crazy," she says. Her hand sweeps back toward the one booth filled with other high school students. Paulie nods at Ron Firth. "And you tip like shit. But relatively speaking, you're probably not crazy. Why do you say that?"

"You can't tell my mom this, okay?"

"And prove she's a better psychologist than you give her credit for?"

"I broke up with Hannah."

"*That's* crazy."

"Wasn't my idea," Paulie says, "but the thing is, I'm, like, kicking myself for bringing it on—when I'm not so mad at her for not listening to me I could scream or punch something."

"Go back to 'bringing it on.'"

"Too long a story," Paulie says. "I don't know, I just wanted to explain myself."

"Would it make a difference?"

Paulie smiles. "Probably not. Good point. Anyway, Arney's been taking her out. . . ."

"What? That inconsiderate shit," Naomi says. "Why don't you kick his ass?"

"I told him okay."

Naomi's look turns stern. "Ask me again if I think you're crazy."

"It's gonna happen with someone; she's Hannah Murphy for chrissake. Might as well be with someone I know."

"That's the dumbest thing I ever heard," Naomi says. "Somebody you *don't* know, you can run into somewhere and pick a fight. It's harder to do with a so-called friend, which by the way if he goes out with Hannah, he isn't. Nobody wants to think about their ex with a *friend*. If I had time I'd tell you a little about *that*."

She's right. Paulie's been shocked awake nightly by the vision of Hannah and Arney in the movie parking lot.

"Maybe you should start hanging out with my Karin. An ambitious young man like you would be good for her."

"I thought Karin was in juvy."

"She should be out in the next couple of weeks, if she'll goddamn behave herself."

"No offense, Naomi, but I'd be terrified to go out with any girl raised by you. I mean that as a compliment."

The cook slides Paulie's onion rings and burger under the heat lamp and Naomi places the plate in front of him just as the bell hanging over the entrance rings and three men walk in and sit several seats down.

"Gotta get to work," Naomi says. "Only other thing I can recommend to a guy in your position is to join up with the Thumpers. Let Jesus find a way." She laughs and nods at a back booth.

"We're not quite a fit," Paulie says, smiling. "I think the answer is to drown my sorrows." He takes a gigantic bite of his burger and washes it down with milkshake. "And remember, you can't tell my mother. She doesn't know any of this. I'll give it to her a little at a time."

Naomi's already taking the three men's orders, but she

runs her fingers across her lips with the zipper sign.

Paulie finishes the burger in four more bites, eats the onion rings two at a time, drains the shake, leaves Naomi a bigger than shit tip, and gets up to go.

"Mr. Bomb!" comes from the back booth.

"Mr. Firth," Paulie says. "Whassup?"

"Just sittin' here rootin' out evil," Ron says. "Come on back."

"Gotta get home," Paulie says. "I just stopped for a little dinner to hold me over 'til dinner. My mom's expecting me."

"Come on, Bomb. Won't hurt you to sit with us and get the Word. We need a little stimulation. Everyone back here agrees with each other. It's boring."

Paulie smiles and walks back.

The booth is full so he sits across the narrow aisle and orders another shake. "So how you guys doin'? Jesus still all right?"

It brings smiles. A couple of kids sitting against the window break briefly into The Doobie Brothers' version.

"From what you said in P-8 the other day, sounds like you could use a little Jesus," Firth says.

Paulie glances up. Things said in Period 8 stay there.

Ron reads his mind. "They don't know what I'm talking

about," he says. "I keep the faith with Mr. Logs."

"I'll give you all dispensation on this one," Paulie says back. "Anybody wants to know the horror of my life can go read Hannah Murphy's Facebook page. She doesn't name names, but it doesn't take a genius to know which a-hole is which."

"Hannah Murphy was talking about *you*?" Cassandra Hoops says. "I thought all that was rhetorical."

Paulie says, "When was the last time you heard Hannah Murphy get rhetorical?"

Carrie Morales says, "So you're an adulterer."

"Just a dick, if you'll pardon the expression," Paulie says. "Nobody involved was married. Or an adult."

"Semantics, really," Carrie says.

"Actually, we have to give our wayward friend the benefit of the doubt here," Ron says. "No promises were made in the presence of God. Let's not get too hardass here, folks, even though it's we who profess to be without sin." He raises his eyebrows at Carrie.

"So there, Carrie Morales," Paulie says.

The others look on as if they need to be brought up to speed.

"I cheated," Paulie says. "And I'm getting what I deserved. Actually, you could have wormed all this out of

Arney Stack. You guys have *his* ear."

Firth says, "Say what?"

"I thought you guys were lobbying Stack to get Johannsen and the school board to let you have a classroom for your get-togethers. Midnight meeting? One of these last Fridays?"

YFC heads shake in unison. "One more politician who doesn't come through," Firth says. "Mr. Stack hasn't been at one of our meetings since we carried the election for him."

"Carried the election." Paulie laughs. "You and every other group in school. Arney didn't meet with you guys a couple Fridays ago?"

"Haven't seen Arney at one of our meetings—formal or informal—since last year."

"And we *sure* haven't seen him at any of the late Friday night meetings," Carrie adds. "Those are where we have some fun. I'd remember that."

Paulie shrugs and runs the business end of his straw around the inside of his glass, sucking up the cold residue like an 8-pound Oreck. "Gotta go, you guys. Thanks for bearing witness."

"You wouldn't have to change much, Mr. Bomb," Ron Firth says, "to be one of us. We have hope for you."

"Thanks anyway," Paulie says back, "but as much time as I spend trying to haul myself through the water, I'm suspicious of guys who walk on it."

"See you in school, man."

Paulie belts himself into the Beetle and sits, staring out the windshield at Frank's Diner. Arney *didn't* have to speed off to YFC that night. Why would he say that? Where was he going that he didn't want Paulie to know? He said in Period 8 that Mary Wells was a friend; why would he not be willing to give her a lift? And Hannah said Arney was the only guy she knew who wasn't afraid of Mary's dad. What's that about?

He jumps at a knock on the driver's-side window, looks up into Mary's face. She motions him to roll down the window. "Can we talk?"

"Jeez! There are forty thousand people in this town, how come I keep running into you?"

She smiles. "No coincidence. I'm stalking you. You drive a lime-green Beetle, Paulie, basically a neon girlie car. You're not that hard to track."

"I don't identify myself by my ride," he says. "What do you want to talk about?"

"Things," Mary says. "Just things."

.10

"I still can't believe he let you go," Arney says. "You guys were like, the perfect couple."

"He didn't let me go," Hannah says. "I dumped him. He cheated and I dumped him."

"Well, then I can't believe he cheated. Who would give you up for, like *anybody*?"

"I guess *he* would. Look, it hurts to talk about it, okay?"

"Still got something for him, huh?" he says. "I just . . ."

"Enough."

"And his choice . . ."

"Arney."

Arney grabs a handful of popcorn and crams it into his mouth as the lights go down for the main feature.

Hannah stares at the screen. "This is a classic," she says. "You know who Alfred Hitchcock was?"

"I'm the one who picked the movie," Arney says through a mouthful of popcorn. "Of course I know who Alfred Hitchcock was. This is like one of his all-timers."

The opening credits to *Psycho* roll.

"What about his choice?" Hannah whispers.

"You said you didn't want to talk about it anymore."

"*What about his choice?* You know who it was?"

"Yeah, I know."

Hannah is quiet.

"Want me to tell you?"

She stares ahead. Arney waits.

"No."

"Guess there's no fixing what happened," Mary Wells says.

"Nothing to fix," Paulie says back. "It happened. It was what it was."

"I'm sorry about you losing Hannah."

Paulie's eyes narrow. "How did you find out I lost Hannah?"

"Everyone in school knows it."

"Who told it to you first? You said it to me before you would have heard it at school."

"Did I? I don't remember where I heard it, Paulie."

"You know what? There's too much mystery here."

"I know," she says. "There are things I can't talk about. Things aren't always how they appear."

"Yeah, but they aren't usually exactly opposite of how they appear, either. I'm a nice guy. Like you said. Not dangerous and all that? But I'm getting tired of this shit and if you wanna talk about *things*, these are the things I'm willing to talk about before I talk about anything else."

"Can we drive?"

Paulie palms the back of his neck in frustration. "What the hell. Yeah, we can drive. But your car. Like you said, I'm too easy to track."

"Who would be tracking you?"

"Nobody I know of," he says, "but I wouldn't have expected you, either."

"I can't believe he lets you drive this," Paulie says as they settle into the Lexus. "If my parents owned this car, it would never leave the garage."

"He doesn't want me to have one of my own," Mary says. "Too much independence."

She pulls into traffic, silent until they're on the freeway, headed to Diamond Lake. Paulie leans back in the passenger's seat, watching the town go by through the side window, letting his mind bounce with the speed of the passing buildings.

"What is your dad going to do when you take off to school?" he asks after a while.

"I don't know," Mary says. "I'm worried about my sister, Becca. Daddy's not happy unless he's controlling something and she'll be all that's left. He'll have trouble with her, though. She's not like me."

Mary takes the reservoir off-ramp and they speed a short distance through farm- and ranchland. "So it's clear you're still not telling me anything useful," Paulie says. "What do *you* want to talk about?"

Mary hesitates. "Is there any reason we couldn't hang out?"

Paulie's head jerks around. "You mean like right now? Tonight?"

"All the time."

Paulie slumps in the seat. "Reasons we couldn't hang out. Lemme see if I can think of some. How about so Hannah Murphy doesn't kick your ass."

Mary's voice goes sultry. "I love it when you talk dirty."

Paulie grimaces. "Jesus, are you crazy?"

"I thought she was spending time with Arney."

"I thought *you* were spending time with Arney."

Mary looks at him quizzically; her face flushes.

"Coffee? A movie?"

Mary shakes her head. "Coffee once."

"That's it?"

"What did you hear?"

Paulie stares at her. "Nothing." He looks away. "Something way different than that. Look, Mary, our history, yours and mine? Not good. And I am *not* interested in getting into anything. Plus, like I said, if Hannah knew it was you—you wanna talk about someone who's not afraid of your dad—she'd be parked in front of your house."

"Believe me, I've been hurt a lot worse than Hannah Murphy could hurt me."

"Christ, Mary, if I *were* interested in a relationship, it wouldn't be with somebody who tells half of everything."

"If I said I'm not afraid of Hannah? Could we hang out then?"

Why can I not get through to you?

"Paulie, I want to be with you. I *need* to be with you."

It's that voice he heard the other night when she wanted to know if she was *good*.

"Are you not listening? Mary, I don't even know you."

She smiles. "You know at least one thing about me," she says. "And you said it wasn't so bad."

Paulie stares straight ahead.

"Come on, Paulie. You don't have to tell anybody we're . . . you know."

"We are *not* 'you know.'"

Mary takes a deep breath. "Then hang out long enough to get to know me," she says. "Then you can decide."

Paulie doesn't answer. He's quiet a few more miles, then, "You know, Mr. Logs says when we don't understand something, it's because we don't have enough information; that there's almost nothing we can't figure out with knowledge. You agree with that?"

"I guess."

"Okay, so I don't understand this. You act all one way, like you're an icon for celibacy. You could be queen of YFC. Then you, like, offer yourself up. I can see you fooling your dad and having maybe a secret relationship with somebody you love and keeping the personal stuff on the down low, but I swear to God it's like you're two different people."

Mary pulls the car into the reservoir parking lot and turns to face Paulie. "I was on something that night I ran into Hannah," she says.

"Something like drugs?"

"Something exactly like drugs," she says. She looks at her lap. "Oxys."

"Oxycodone? Are you shitting me? Where did *you* get oxys? And *why?* That shit will kill you."

"I know, I know," she says. "It was stupid. I still don't even know how I got to Hannah's house. I barely remember getting into her car."

"Who gave you that shit, Mary?"

"I can't tell you that. I know what you'd do, and it was my fault. It was just once. I haven't taken anything since. And I won't. I promise." She leans back in the seat. "So can we?"

"Hang out?"

"Yes."

"We can talk, Mary, but we are *not* together and we are not messing around. Despite what Justin Chenier says about guys, I don't play. Not anymore." He turns sideways, facing her with his back as far against the door as the seat belt will allow. "And you avoided my question.

I asked about you being two different people, you said you were on oxys the night Hannah found you, not the night you were all over me."

Mary grips the wheel. "Listen." Her voice is serious, almost aggressive. "If I get another shot at you I'm going to take it. And I'll teach you things you haven't even thought of. Plant *that* in your brain." She drops her arms. "But if I can't have that, I need you to do something for me."

Fuck. "I don't even know why I'm asking, but what?"

"I need you to make it *look* serious. Nothing has to happen."

"I'm *not* going to make it look serious. People think I'm enough of an asshole as it is."

The desperation returns to Mary's voice. "Then make it look like it *could* be. Down the road. I know I'm going to make you mad again because I can't tell you why, but it's almost life or death."

"Give me a fucking break. Life or death for *who?*"

Mary simply shakes her head.

As he watches Mary drive away, Paulie drops into the driver's seat of his Beetle, lays the seat all the way back, and stares at the ceiling, one leg in and one leg out of the car. *What is fucking* wrong *with me? I'm talking to Mary Wells like she didn't just ruin my life. Can we hang out? Can we fucking hang out?* He takes a deep breath. *The answer is no, you dumb asshole, not "we can talk, but blah blah blah." It's NO!* He hits the back of his head softly against the headrest. *But Hannah and Arney . . . God*damn!

He brings the seat back up, closes the door, and starts the engine. *Nothing to lose* is not a good place for him to be.

"Tell me where I went wrong."

Mary Wells drops her backpack onto the bar in the dining room and sits on a stool in front of it. "You didn't go wrong, Mom. It had nothing to do with you."

"Nothing to do with me? You're my daughter. You're months—*weeks*—away from graduation and you disappear. Everything you've worked for is in jeopardy and you disappear for days. I've asked you over and over and you give me nothing. Do I seem that foolish to you? You've never done *anything* like that. We thought we'd gotten you through these awful high school years unscarred and then . . . *this*."

You didn't get me through these awful high school years, Mary thinks. *You made these high school years awful. If you knew how much I hate you, you'd kill yourself.*

"It's over now, Mom. Everything you guys wanted for me will happen. I'll work it out with Daddy. There's nothing to worry about."

"I hope so," Miriam Wells says. "These last few weeks have been the hardest in my life. Do you have any idea what you've put us through? Think of your sister." She begins to tear up.

Mary closes her eyes. This is the part of her mother that drives her crazy: always making things look some way they're not. *You know your father loves you, he just doesn't know how to show it. If he didn't care, he wouldn't get so angry.* Always worried more about how things look than how they are. In the dark of her room late at night, in her best moments of clarity, Mary watches herself turn into that person.

"You should have heard your dad after the Father/ Daughter Prom. He said you were the prettiest girl there. He said you were the *one* girl who he *knew* would keep her promise of chastity until marriage, the one girl who would never disappoint her father in any way. All those cute little religious girls with their high necklines and crosses . . . they had nothing on you."

Mary looks away. *Never disappointing your father is NOT who a girl needs to be, you stupid bitch! Half the time he wants me sexy and the other half he wants a goddamn three-year-old! He's SICK! YOU'RE sick! I'M sick!!!* She closes her eyes. She can get through this. There is no reason for her mother to ever know. She has two cell phones now: one to give her dad at the end of the day and one that holds the answers to the mysteries of her recent history. She's nowhere to be found on the Internet other than her cheerleader blogs and sweet "hi-ya" emails. *There HAS to be a way out.* Before this year she thought it was college, but it's going to be more drastic.

"You didn't break *that* vow, did you?"

Yes, Mom, I threw my entire self at Paul Baum. I trapped him. He couldn't get away, and in the end he didn't want to get away. And he wasn't even close to being the first. . . .

"Celibacy? No, Mom, I didn't break that vow." Her life has become so convoluted that lies roll off her tongue like honey.

"You know there are going to be consequences."

Her mother's voice is fading. In fact, her mother's voice has always been faded. It has no weight. It barely has sound. And Mary can hear hers fading with it.

The following afternoon after school, Paulie digs into his backpack for his laptop and places it gently on the tabletop at The Rocket, hoping for divine inspiration. He's always done his best thinking in the white noise of a small restaurant or coffee shop and this one has the advantage of feeling like his home away from home. His bedroom is for sleep. His senior thesis is due *soon* and he has been swimming, working here, and playing rat basketball and screwing up his life instead of getting it written. So far, he has the title—ADOLESCENT DECISION-MAKING— and about fifty opening sentences. His idea when he chose the topic was to focus on information he'd gathered from his psychology class, brain science books, the news, and personal experience. Mr. Logs is his thesis advisor, selected because he'd get "latitude," but also because he knew Logs would hold his feet to the fire to get a quality product. He wants that: a quality product. There has been a whole lot of high school for which he has little respect. Testing his memory 'til it was sore and bleeding has never held much water for him and the rah-rah of sports and school loyalty hasn't cranked him up much, though he roots for the school's teams and wears the colors on occasion. But Logs has always said *this* is the time. "You want to come out of high school at full speed," Logs says. "Too many people pass it off as time spent waiting for your real life to start.

But it doesn't have to be. The more you know about what lies out there the further ahead you are when you step out."

Much as he respects Logs, "stepping out ahead" isn't the main objective. Paulie wants to understand the life he's living now. He wants to know his possibilities, his *edges*. Now.

Paulie wishes sometimes he had Arney's ability to detach, to see things in his mind instead of in his heart, and to just take what he wants. He looks at his title page. *Why does it seem like I have a choice between so many good decisions while Bobby and Taylor—and a whole bunch of other kids—have to choose between the shitty ones?*

He steps behind the counter to put a sixteen-ounce coffee and a scone on his tab, then returns to the small table where he's plugged in his laptop, cracking his knuckles, ready to get some *words* down. He opens a manila folder containing notes from *Brain Rules* and *How We Decide*, some Internet printouts of teenagers doing heroic things and mind-numbingly stupid things. He could keep all that information in his laptop, but he wants it where he can pull it out of his backpack at any time.

He types, absently finishing the scone, hoping for the wisdom that sometimes comes with a caffeine rush.

"Hey, man."

He looks up. "Justin. 'Sup?"

"All lonely and shit," Justin says. "Saw the lime-green Beetle and thought I'd come in and see if I can keep you from graduating."

Paulie closes the laptop. "Who needs a diploma anyway," he says. "Studies say the job I want won't even exist by the time I get my education and it will only require a GED anyway. I can go straight to welfare."

"*That's* the man I backed for prez," Justin says. "A little more of that kind of rhetoric and your campaign might'a got off the ground."

"We gave it our best shot. Pretty glad I didn't win."

Justin's fingers tap nonstop on the table to some driving beat playing in his head. "You know, bro, your opponent was low-down. He's still low-down."

"Arney? I guess. He was just being Arney."

"Yeah, and I let that go. Politics and all, and you seemed okay with it. But that personal shit trash-talking your pops and all that DNA stuff was out of line."

"I straightened him out on that," Paulie says. "He still claims he didn't know beforehand. And he stopped it."

"Tell you what, my man, there is *damn* little happens around Mr. Stack he doesn't know about."

"Did you come here just to cheer me up?"

Justin looks behind him at the entrance, then back at Paulie. "I came here to *smarten* you up," he says. "This shit with Stack and Hannah ain't right."

"I know. I gave him the go-ahead, though," Paulie says. "Can you imagine what Hannah Murphy would say if she thought somebody needed *permission* to go out with her? Especially mine?"

"He asked because he knew what you'd say. Man, you act all tough and shit but I know what's going on inside. Stack can see it too, man, and he uses it. That's what pisses me off, it's fucked up."

"I'll get through it. Shit, kids are starvin' in Somalia."

"Which at this particular moment in our lives we can do zero about," Justin says. "Arney, however, is more *immediate*."

Paulie smiles and leans back. "Well, I can't go busting up Arney because I don't like him going out with my ex-girlfriend. She's got a part in it, too."

"She's getting even, like any chick would. I'll give her that room, but if Stack was ever my friend, it's history now."

"Well, if it elevates your opinion of my sanity," Paulie says, "I'm cooling off on him, too."

"Just know if you're laying around some night feelin'

like destroying some property, give me a call."

A quick fist bump and Justin turns to leave. Paulie watches him disappear through the door. Justin whirls and points and Paulie hears a muffled, "Got your back, man," through the window. Justin walks a couple more steps, whirls and points again, and mouths, "But whose got your front?"

Paulie opens the laptop again, sighs, and tries to focus, only to look up and see Hannah standing at the counter. His adrenaline floodgates open: quick heartbeats and an ache in his lower back, and he moves to the opposite side of the table facing away.

He wants to write his goddamn paper, but he can't concentrate until he knows she's gone, so he pretends to read, counting out the seconds he thinks it will take them to make a double-shot vanilla latte. She was texting; he doesn't know if she saw him and he's pretty sure if she did, she'll pretend otherwise. When the bell hanging over the door rings three more times, he ventures a look over his shoulder.

Hannah stands two feet away. "Hey," she says.

"We have to stop meeting like this."

She says, "Funny."

"Not much material to work with."

"Were you ever going to tell me?"

"Tell you what?"

"Who you cheated with."

The bottom drops out of Paulie's stomach. "What do you mean *was* I ever going to tell you? You know?"

"Yeah, I know."

He closes his eyes. He *told* Mary not to try to fix things.

"When did she tell you?"

"*She* didn't. Paulie, how could you do that?"

His mind spins. He doesn't know from which direction this attack is coming, or from which to attack back.

"Do what?"

"Take advantage of someone like Mary Wells. I thought I knew you."

"How can I put this delicately," Paulie says. "Who the fuck told you it was Mary Wells?"

"That's none of your business."

"It sure as hell is my business, because only two people knew."

"Obviously that's not true, and you still haven't answered my question."

He closes his laptop, folds his hands on the table. "You know, Hannah, I'd answer your question, I would. But it wouldn't do a bit of good. Your mind's made up about me.

I'm my old man and that's it. Well, tell you what. I ain't my old man and until you clear your pretty little head out so you can hear what's what, all I can say is fuck off."

"Have it your way," she says.

"That possibility dried up the day I told you the truth," he says back.

"That possibility dried up the day you did it."

He grits his teeth. "Whatever. Do me one favor, though, and then I promise, I'll never darken your door again, literally or figuratively. Tell me who said it was Mary. Better. I'll make it easy. I'll say the name and if I'm right, don't say anything."

Hannah shrugs.

"It was fucking Arney, wasn't it?"

Hannah flushes slightly and stares straight at him.

"Thanks. Now you have a latte to drink and I have a paper to write. If you're gonna stay here to drink it, I'll pack my shit and go. If not I'd appreciate it if you'd get us out of each other's faces."

"On my way," Hannah says.

.11

Paulie drops his gym bag next to the bleachers and scans the six half-courts, looking for the right open-gym game. Justin and a couple of his buddies hold the court next to the entrance and Justin motions him over. "Will's got to get with his honey," he says. "Play with us."

"Tell Will to hang on for one more game and I'll be back," Paulie says, and moves two courts down where Arney plays with two first-stringers from the high school team. On the adjacent court, Sam Jackson, another first-stringer, shoots jumpers.

"Got winners?" Paulie asks.

Jackson nods.

"I go with you?"

Sam passes him the ball. "Sure. Get warm."

Minutes later, after Arney's team wins, Paulie says, "Let's do it."

They pick up the best shooter from the losing team, Randy Wilkes, and take the court.

"Hey, bud," Arney says. "Ready to get schooled?"

"Hey, bud," Paulie says back. Arney misses the irony.

Rules say winner's outs, so Arney's team takes the ball. "I got the prez," Paulie says, and Sam and Randy square off with the others. Arney passes in to his big man, Ronnie Turner, who fires it back and cuts to the hoop. Arney fakes the pass and pops a jumper, looking Paulie in the eye just before he releases.

Enjoy it, Paulie thinks.

It's Arney's last point. Paulie is on him like a wetsuit, slapping the ball out of his hands at every opportunity, blocking him from passes. Arney grows exasperated and throws the ball away twice, which gets Turner on his case. "Come on, prez. Don't force it, man. Take your time. He's got size on you. You got to play smart."

But Paulie's anger works to his advantage; he's seeing Arney's moves before Arney makes them, crowding his left side because Arney's a southpaw, forcing everything the other way. He can feel Arney's frustration building.

Paulie plays psychologically sweet, complimenting Arney when he almost pulls off a move, encouraging him to stay with it. "I'm fresh," Paulie says. "You'll wear me down pretty soon."

"Yeah," Arney says, "like *any*body could wear *you* down."

"You're having an off night," Paulie says, and slaps the ball into the bleachers.

"Man, what's with you?" Arney says.

"Just workin' out the kinks of a *bad* day," Paulie says back.

Turner says, "Will you girls shut up and play?"

Paulie smiles and nods. He will most certainly shut up and play.

Arney passes the ball in and cuts to the hoop, circling under the backboard and out to the corner baseline, with Paulie tracking every step. Paulie's teammates are emboldened by his defense and turn it up on their end. Arney cuts back toward the hoop on the baseline and Paulie lets him go, giving his big man just enough room to sneak in a bounce pass. Arney goes up for the shot with Paulie right behind him, his palm on the ball and no part of their bodies touching. He slams the ball back into Arney's face, sending him sprawling across the floor. Blood squirts from Arney's nose.

"My foul," Paulie says. "You guys' ball." He offers Arney his hand.

Arney slaps it away. "Jesus, Baum, what the fuck is the matter with you? You had the block."

"Guess I got too into it," Paulie says. "Sorry, man."

Turner says, "You okay, prez?"

Arney wipes his nose with his hand, sees blood. "I'm okay, but I'm done. I'm not playing with this asshole."

Turner glances around the gym. "We need a third."

Paulie walks to the sideline. "That's okay. I'll call it, too. You guys go two-on-two."

Without turning back he moves to call winners on Justin's court.

Arney Stack walks in his back door, through the kitchen, and heads for the stairs toward his room. His mother intercepts him at the base of the stairway, seeing crusted blood below his swollen nose. "What in the world happened to you?"

"Basketball," he says. "It got a little rough."

His father appears in the entrance to the living room. A thin, wiry man, impeccably dressed even in his casuals. "Let me look at that."

Arney grimaces and approaches his father. "Yes, sir."

Arnold Sr. studies the wound. "Did you extract retribution?"

"Naw, it was Paulie."

"I see. An accident?"

Arney smiles. "Not exactly. He was irritated at me from something at school."

"Having to do with the Murphy girl?"

Arney takes a deep breath. "I don't know. Probably."

"So he takes it out on you on the court."

"I guess."

"And you do nothing."

"It was Paulie, Dad." He doesn't say that Paulie was so pissed he'd have retributed the retribution in a big way, but makes it sound like he gave his friend a pass.

The open-palmed slap to the side of Arney's face knocks him back two steps. He catches himself on the banister.

His mother retreats, hand over her mouth.

"You're a Stack," his father says, low and mean. "*No* one assaults a Stack and walks away, understood? Especially that Baum kid. He's diminished you all your life." It's his father's favorite word. *Diminished*.

Arney is *physically* strong enough to take his dad, but he says, "Yes, sir."

"You give a man an advantage and he takes advantage."

"Yes, sir. No excuse."

"Very well, then. I'm sorry I had to strike you."

"I had it coming, sir. You're right. I can't pick a fight, but you can rest assured I'll get him back, and he'll know it."

A slight smile crosses his father's face. "You're a good man, son. Or you will be."

The following afternoon Paulie drives slowly toward the Wells mansion, his mind bouncing over what to say when he gets there. "Make it look like we're hanging out," he says to the steering wheel. "Hi, Mr. Wells. I'm Paul Baum. Your daughter and I had a quick one in my car a little while back, but that's over now and I'm here to make it *look like* she and I are hanging out. Don't go for your firearms, it's all for show." He laughs. What the fuck. *I'm ninety percent sure*, he thinks, *but I need a hundred: did Arney tell Hannah?*

"Can I help you?" Victor Wells looks bigger in the door

of his mansion than he did in the park, and every bit as intimidating.

"Yes, sir. Is Mary here?"

"She's here but I'm afraid she isn't taking callers."

"This is about school," Paulie says.

"Is she expecting you?"

Funny, Paulie thinks. *Name two guys she has ever expected to come here.*

"I don't think so. It's about a project we're working on."

"She hasn't mentioned a project. Is this recent?"

"Actually it's old. We started it at the beginning of the semester and I've been procrastinating." For an avowed truth-teller, this lying stuff comes way too easy.

Wells's eyes narrow. "Didn't I meet you at the park when school kids were out looking for my daughter?"

"Maybe. I mean, you could have. We were all out there."

Wells studies Paulie's face, which Paulie holds devoid of expression. "I suppose she can give you a few minutes, but make it short."

"Yes, sir."

"Wait here."

Paulie stands on the porch, taking in the surroundings.

The porch wraps completely around the house like on a southern antebellum mansion, the lawn perfectly manicured.

"She says she can't talk with you right now," Wells says upon his quick return.

"Could you tell her it's really important?" Paulie's heart pounds against his breastbone. Wells was gone but a few seconds; Paulie doesn't trust that he actually asked her.

"Son, I'm formally asking you to leave my property. I'm sure you don't want me to call security."

"You have security? Why in the world would you need security?"

"That's none of your damn business. Now get off my porch."

Paulie takes a deep breath. "Mr. Wells, I'm not a bad guy. I'm not here to cause trouble or do harm to your daughter. I'm asking you—I'm begging you—to tell her it's really important, that it won't take more than five minutes and we can have the conversation right here on the porch. It could affect my graduation."

"Boy, you've got some nerve."

"Thank you, sir."

"I didn't mean it as a compliment."

"C'mon. Five minutes."

Wells disappears again and Paulie starts to sweat. It's as if he's starting a four-mile swim in shark-infested waters.

"Hey," Mary says, coming down the stairs. "What are you doing here?" Her demeanor tells him he was right: Wells didn't tell her he was here the first time.

"I need to talk with you about our project," Paulie says, guarding against the possibility that her father is behind the door.

"Want me to get my notes?"

She's a quick study. "Yeah, sure." He's been here only ten minutes, and already has a sense of extreme vigilance.

Mary hurries to her room, grabs a notebook, hurries back. She steps onto the porch, closing the front door behind her.

"Jesus Christ," Paulie says.

"Sit next to me," Mary whispers. "If he asks, it's civics. He knows which classes I take at school and which I take for Running Start, but he wouldn't know you and I aren't in the same civics class." The notebook is open to early semester notes, focused on actions by the Supreme Court. "We're working on the court's decision to treat corporations as individuals," she says, "a decision he likes a lot. I'm writing advantages and you're doing disadvantages."

"This is like a *test*."

"And you need to get an A on it. My dad has radar for lies, and you can bet he's a lot better at flushing them out than you are at telling them." She smiles. "Especially you, Paulie."

"Man, how do you live like this?"

"I just try to stay on his good side," she says. "When we're done talking, go straight to your car. Don't say good-bye or engage him in any way or he'll get you talking and if you make a mistake, the hammer comes down on me."

Paulie closes his eyes and sighs.

"Stare at the notebook and take that look off your face," she says. She turns the page. "We don't have much time, so tell me why you came."

"I need to know something."

"What?"

"And if the answer's yes, it's okay with me. I ain't judgin' nobody for nothin', thanks partly to you, so there's no cost to this."

"*What?*"

"Did you tell Hannah that you and I—"

"No!"

"Did you tell Arney?"

She tells a lie that isn't exactly a lie. "No."

"I'm serious, Mary. It would be okay—"

"No."

"Okay, one more. I know you think you answered this before, but did you guys have something going?"

Mary stares at the porch floor. Almost inaudibly she says, "No."

"I've heard several people say he's the one guy in the world—or at least the one teenage guy—who isn't scared of your dad."

"Arney and I did some community service stuff together for our college resumes. He's picked me up here a few times. As long as it's daylight . . ."

The front door opens. Victor Wells fills the entranceway. "Are you two about finished?"

"Yes, Daddy. Just a couple more minutes." She laughs lightly. "Paulie is about three months behind on a project we have to turn in in time to be graded for the semester."

"Two minutes," her father says and moves back inside. Mary stands and pulls the door closed.

"You have anything for him?"

"Arney?"

"Yeah."

"Uh-huh. I hate his guts."

"Care to elaborate?"

Mary looks at the ground. "No."

Fuck. "Okay. For now. So listen, if I decide we can do this charade . . . hang out . . ." He nods toward the house. "How do I get past that?"

"Do everything from school." She looks back at the door. "Go."

"One sec." Paulie stands and pushes open the door. "Thanks so much, Mr. Wells. You may have saved my life." Then he is down the walk and in his car.

Two days later, Paulie and Justin pop jumpers in the gym after school. "Arney came askin' about you."

"Yeah?"

"Says you took him out on purpose the other night."

"Came onto my ground," Paulie says. "Just like you, he's got no business driving on me. Had to teach him some respect."

"Onto your ground in more ways than one," Justin says.

"Yeah, well, I guess I didn't know how pissed I was until I saw him struttin' his shit with those varsity guys."

"Man, you got to get off this passive-aggressive stuff and just get aggressive. Arney's playing the victim because you said Hannah was fair game when you really meant better stay the fuck away." Justin starts to drive, pulls up, and bangs a high one off the front rim. He snags the rebound, dribbles behind his back, and charges to hoop as if to dunk, going through the motion even though at the height of his leap he's four inches below the rim.

"That was about a foot short of a Blake Griffin!" Paulie says. "Give you an eight for form, though."

"Doc says I may be in for a late growth spurt."

"Uh-huh. Listen, Jus, Hannah's stuff aside, something is *way* whack with Arney."

"Like I haven't been telling you that? How do you mean?"

"The lies are stacking up, no pun intended. First he says he's going to a midnight meeting with the Thumpers when I needed him to do me a favor, but Firth tells me he hasn't talked to him outside of class or P-8 since the election last year. Then he goes out of his way to tell us all he's got some inside track on Mary Wells, how she's different than everyone thinks and how her old man ain't so bad, and I find out that's bullshit, too."

Justin frowns. "How'd you find out *that*?"

"Never mind."

"Naw, man, you confide *some* of this shit, you got to confide it *all.*"

Paulie feeds him as he breaks to the hoop again. Justin stops, whirls, and buries a short jumper.

"More like it," Paulie says.

"Spill it."

"Okay, man, but if I confide it, it's exactly that: confidential."

"I ever rat you out?"

"You've never had anything to rat."

"Man, you are *killing* me."

Paulie stops, holds the ball under his arm. "Nah, man, you know I'd trust you with anything."

"Show me some proof."

Paulie closes his eyes, shakes his head and lets out big air. "Mary is who I cheated on Hannah with. Bro, you can't tell *anyone.*" He passes Justin the ball.

Justin spikes it with both hands and sits on it. "You did the Virgin Mary?"

Paulie sits down beside him, lays back on the floor, shielding his eyes from the afternoon sunlight pouring through a high window. "No, I didn't *do* the Virgin Mary. I . . . it's a long story."

"Like to have *that* on my resume," Justin says. "How'd you pull it off?"

"It wasn't my idea."

Justin smiles. "I *thought* there was more to that girl."

"Whatever you thought, you didn't get it right," Paulie says. "Look, after it happened, she didn't want anyone to know. You know I didn't tell because you would have been the first. But Hannah comes up to me in The Rocket and says she knows who it was. And she gets it right. Far as I know, two people knew: Mary and me. I sure as *hell* didn't tell Hannah and she says she didn't hear it from a *she*. Who's Hannah been hanging with? Stack. I take my life in my hands and go over to Mary's place, almost lost a body part getting past her old man, but I gotta be sure. I mean, I *believed* Hannah 'cause, well, I believe Hannah, but I wanted two good sources. Mary says no way she told Hannah. But she says she didn't tell Arney, either. *Somehow,* Arney knows. He couldn't just have guessed. I mean, how many guesses would you make before you picked Mary Wells?"

"All of 'em," Justin says. "This is some *intrigue*." He

stands, twirling the ball on his index finger. It spins off and lands on Paulie's gut.

"No shit." Paulie grunts, sitting up with the ball between his legs. "Arney's involved in this some way I don't get."

"Involved in what? You have a conspiracy theory?"

"Maybe. Shit, I don't know."

"Man, you should finish out the year at the alternative school. Stay away from all this shit."

"No kidding. And then there's Mary's dad. Man, he is a whole other thing. Either she stays five moves ahead of him or . . . I don't know what. That girl is under siege. You ever do soft eyes, Jus?"

A rapid shake of the head. "What's that?"

"You know, when you're looking too hard at some problem—like even in calc—you just let everything go unfocused and things that are supposed to go together, do?"

Justin shakes his head again. "I go hard eyes in calc," he says. "Best way to see Marley's answers."

Paulie knows he's kidding. Justin Chenier would cheat at *nothing*, particularly in calc, where all eyes would be on *his* paper.

"When I go soft eyes on all this," Paulie says, "Mary's

old man comes floating right to the center. But so does Stack."

Justin squints. "So this Virgin Mary thing, you *involved?*"

Paulie looks away. "Not really, at least not in the way you're talking about. I didn't have sex with Mary Wells because I wanted to. . . ."

"You didn't have sex with her because you *didn't* want to."

"It's a long story, Jus, and way over your head."

"Best you hit the water with the Log man tomorrow. This is the kind of shit you take to a *pro.*"

.12

"Hey, asshole, we need to talk."

Paulie walks toward his car following last period. It's Friday afternoon and he's looking forward to a hard swim. He turns to face Arney. "So talk."

"What was that bullshit on the court the other night?" Arney says.

"I told you before," Paulie says back, "don't bring that weak shit into the paint on me."

"You could have just wrapped me up."

"You got around me. I wasn't going to give you a cheap one."

"It's rat ball, for chrissake," Arney says. "And I'll tell you what, buddy, it felt personal."

Paulie leans against the Beetle. "You're right, Arney. It was personal. It was about you and Hannah and all the bullshit you've been throwing . . . like since the third grade."

"You said—"

"I know what I said, and it's too late to un-say it. But I never would have done that to you. Wouldn't have even asked. I wouldn't have done it to Hannah, either. I've got too much chivalry to take *her* out on the court, so you got the lucky draw, okay? Besides, she's tougher than you, so it was less risky."

Arney looks down. "You're right, man. I'm sorry. I'll stop—"

"Fuck that," Paulie says. "That genie doesn't fit back into the bottle. She looks different to me than she did a week ago anyway. I'll just stay away from you guys."

"Listen . . ."

"Listen, my ass. I've figured you out, Stack. You try shit 'til something works. You asked me about you and Hannah and I said 'go ahead' when I meant 'what the fuck' because I figured I screwed Hannah over and I don't deserve a break. But see, you know that about me, Arney. You knew what I'd say. You also knew what a kick in the gut it would be. So when I finally man up and say the truth, you act surprised. Fuckin' Alfred E. Stack. What, me an asshole?"

"It wasn't my idea," Arney says. "Hannah was the one—"

"You're doin' it now, you dick. Hannah's tough, but she's not mean, and she knows she could crush me a lot of ways without going after one of my so-called *friends*. I know you've said some shit to her you wouldn't say to me. She's hanging out with you and there may be some good feeling of revenge to it, but she didn't invent this. You're lucky she and I aren't talking because she'd figure you out pretty quick and this shit would be over."

Arney's hands go up. "Look, man, I'm just trying to find a way to preserve our friendship. We've known each other since we were kids. We can't let some chick—"

"Hannah Murphy's not 'some chick.'"

"You know what I mean."

"I do know what you mean. Tell you what, go home and write down all the shit you've told me in the last few weeks that I might *know* is a lie. I don't know it all yet, but it's getting clearer every day."

Arney swells up, and his expression turns to stone. "Have it your way, *buddy*. Maybe this is the day we cut bait. You want to think twice before calling me a liar."

That's the Arney I was looking for. "I'm way past thinking twice."

Arney takes a step forward. He's not as tall as Paulie and certainly not in as good shape, but he spends hours in the weight room and he could make it interesting.

Paulie doesn't budge. "You know the one comfort I've always had with our 'friendship'?"

"Enlighten me."

"That if it ever comes down to it, I'll just kick your ass. Go for it."

Arney holds his gaze a long moment and Paulie thinks, *This is gonna feel good,* but Arney deflates, then turns for his car. He stops and turns back. "Tell you something else, *buddy.* If I *am* lying, you want to be real careful of what I'm lying *about.* You could be bringing a real shit storm down on a lot of people." He gets into his driver's seat and slams the door.

"Hey, Logs," Paulie says as he and Logs unload their gear. "Remember the other day in P-8 when you started to tell us how your whole perspective changed in the late sixties?"

"I remember."

"Somebody interrupted you. You never finished."

The sky is gray, the temperature chilly as they pull on

their wetsuits. "December '68," Logs says. "First moonshot; the one before we actually landed. Apollo Eight, I think. Practice run to see if we could get them up and back."

"Sixty-eight. Long time ago."

"In a land far away," Logs says. "We'd never seen Earth from a distance. We had drawings, maps, all that, but no one had actually seen us from out there. Those guys were watching *Earth rise.* Or set, I don't know which. It was bigger than the imagination of the entire species.

"I remember thinking, *that's a God's-eye view.* God doesn't see the shit that's going on, He just sees this thing He gave us to live on, and it's beautiful from that far out. He wouldn't even know how badly we messed it up until it was too late; until it turned brown."

It's hard to imagine. Paulie has seen deep space pictures all his life.

"It was something. I mean, now we have the Hubble so we not only see great distances, but back in time. But that first look . . . why you asking?"

"Aw, you know, just like to see an old guy go back."

"Don't mess with me, grasshopper. They'll find you at the bottom of the lake."

"I like that perspective," Paulie says. "You look at

someone and you see the crust, just what the light hits. Kinda the same thing."

"What's driving this?"

"I went over to the Wellses place the other day."

"Whoa."

"No shit, whoa," Paulie says. "Man, Mr. Logs, old man Wells has her vigilant as a prairie dog in a pack of coyotes. You look at him, you don't see it. Watch her *around* him though, and there's no doubt. She could be telling you who really killed President Kennedy and from two feet away look like she's asking about the weather. Always gauging what might set him off. Mary Wells is not who we see."

Logs is almost into his wetsuit. "Tell me that you are not exploring this romantically."

Paulie pulls up his back zipper, reaches into the Beetle for his goggles. He stops. "Logs, is there any way for men and women, or boys and girls, to do *anything* that doesn't turn sexual?"

"I suppose," Logs says, "if a man and a woman drive into an intersection, both talking to their sweethearts on cell phones, paying *no* attention to where they're going, and crash into each other, that possibly isn't sexual. If either one gets out of their car, it's sexual."

"Got it."

"So, about Mary."

"I'm not getting out of the car." Paulie smiles.

"Do you know the term *rebound*, as it's *not* applied in the game of basketball?"

"Yessir, I do."

"And do you remember saying that whole encounter with her was *strange?*"

"I have almost total recall, Sensei."

Logs says, "Prove it."

"Relax. It isn't like that."

"You do *not* want Victor Wells catching you with her," Logs says.

"I know that, believe me." Paulie stops a second. "You don't think there's something going on between *him* and her."

"You mean something inappropriate."

"Hell," Paulie says, "what's happened in the last three weeks that's appropriate? I mean, like, sexual."

"I do not think about things like that if I can help it," Logs says. "It's easy to get suspicious but real dangerous to project. I've learned to respond only to hard evidence, and there isn't any, Paulie, unless you know something you're not telling me."

"I don't, but I have cable. He treats her like *property,*

man. Look, you've been teaching forty-plus years, so you probably see *all* this from the moon, right? I mean, I get that you'd have to say to me or anyone else that you don't *think* something, but your experience *has to* make you consider a lot of things."

"Let me just say this. I have no idea what goes on in the Wells household. What I do know is if you're going to accuse someone like Victor Wells of *jaywalking*, you're already at a disadvantage. A guy with a house like his has at least three lawyers with houses just as big. So, if you want to hang out with Mary Wells, you do it like a recent graduate of etiquette school. You don't honk when you pick her up, you act the perfect gentleman and you keep her out of trouble with him. If something happens that makes you suspicious, I'll be here."

"Thanks," Paulie says. "You want to be real careful around her dad. At least *I* do. And I am *not* getting physical."

Logs rolls his eyes. "I don't know why you don't stay far away, my friend. You're going to do what you do, but just know, control freaks *always* make me nervous. I don't think he's *dangerous*, but as long as he has a grip on her, he can sure make her life miserable, and yours by association." Logs walks to the end of the dock, then turns around. "You know, Paulie, every time you see somebody wounded or in some kind of trouble, you think you have to do something about it. I've always admired that about you. But sometimes there's nothing you can do, and sometimes you can make it worse. Just a thought." He pulls his goggles down. "Now let's get wet."

Paulie stands on the porch of the Wells mansion, hair still wet, once again face-to-face with Victor Wells. "Is Mary home?"

Wells takes a deep breath. "Is she expecting you?"

"I would guess not," Paulie says.

"More of your *project?*" His tone tells Paulie he didn't buy the story last time, or he's discovered some hole in it. Or he has Mary chained down in the basement after burning the truth out of her with lighted cigarettes.

"No, sir," Paulie says. "This is more . . . social."

Wells stiffens. "That's not something we're doing these days."

Paulie smiles. "I wasn't thinking of going anywhere with *you.* Mary."

Wells stares.

"That was a joke."

"Son, you seem like an okay kid, as kids go. But you are barking up the wrong tree if you're thinking about starting something with my daughter. She's had some problems, as I'm sure you're aware, and we're focusing on straightening things out and getting on with life, which means college and *preparation* for college. That's a full plate right now."

Paulie takes a deep breath; he's rehearsed this. "Look, sir, with all due respect, I'm not trying to start something. I was thinking of, like, ice cream or coffee."

"I don't think you understand."

"Mr. Wells, do you know you're famous?"

"Excuse me?"

"You're famous."

"Probably I am," Wells says with a grimace. "I certainly made a splash the past couple of weeks in the media, jumping the gun on Mary's 'disappearance.'" He looks to the side.

"That's not why you're famous."

Wells' irritation is evident. "Okay, then why am I famous?"

"You're like a *legend*," Paulie says, "and not in a good way. I mean, you wanna know how kids talk about somebody who's *always* in control? You're, like, a teenager's idea of a monster."

Paulie notices the muscle at the top of Wells's jaw turn into a small marble.

"Did you come here just to flatter me?" Wells says.

"I came with an offer," Paulie says. "Look, I'm an almost-eighteen-year-old kid who doesn't drink or smoke or take drugs. I have a B average, give or take a minus or two, and I am headed to the U next year. My grade average indicates I'm something of an underachiever, but I test well. I just got dumped by a girl I was on my a— I was over the top for and I'm not about to get into more mess. I have a father who plays around and that hacks me off, and a mother who allows it, which hacks me off even more. I take care of my body and I tell the truth whenever I can. I'm totally aware that if I spend any time with your daughter, you'll check all that out and if I'm lying, you'll know it before I come around again."

"You tell the truth whenever you can?"

"Yeah, like with important things. Like, I wouldn't tell you how dorky it looks to wear dark nylon socks with those shorts." He nods toward Wells's feet.

Wells follows Paulie's gaze and for the first time in the conversation, smiles.

"So your daughter would be relatively safe and you'd

buy some good will with kids at school, which probably doesn't matter to you one way or the other."

"Relatively safe."

"We're teenagers, Mr. Wells. We live in risky times."

Wells stares at Paulie. "You are one ballsy young man."

"You almost have to be these days," Paulie says.

Wells turns and the door closes. Paulie shuts his eyes as he hears him call to his daughter. "Mary, you have a visitor."

Paulie touches the soaked shirt under his arm.

"You called my father a dork?" Mary is amazed; just a little too scared to think it's funny, but close.

"Technically I didn't call him that. I said the socks were dorky. He may have extrapolated from that." Paulie is smiling, feeling triumphant. "He got even, though," Paulie says.

"How?"

"He gave me one of those looks."

"Yeah," Mary says, "he can do that. At least you got to his sense of humor."

"So, you're on furlough. What do you want to do?"

"He didn't give us a lot of time. Jeez, a ten thirty curfew

on a Friday night. What other seventeen-year-old girl has that?"

"Probably the YFC girls," Paulie says, "but most of theirs are probably self-imposed."

Mary smiles. "I know a lot of those girls," she says. "They believe in what they believe, but that doesn't always translate into what they do."

"Justin claims biology trumps everything."

"Speaking of biology," Mary says, placing a hand on Paulie's thigh, "we could go—"

"Not gonna happen."

"I want to give you something to thank you. . . ."

"Not gonna happen."

"I want to."

The picture of taking Mary to the secret room at the strip mall begins immediately to cloud Paulie's judgment, but the thought of being with Mary in the same place he was with Hannah. . . . "Not gonna happen."

"I'm not asking you to fall in love with me, Paulie. You're not with anyone and neither am I. What's the harm?"

"The harm isn't anything I would know about until it happens to me," Paulie says. "Look, I've got flash photos of Arney-fucking-Stack and Hannah going off in my head every hour on the hour, and I'll tell you the truth, I'm hanging with you partly as a 'fuck you' to them. I'll probably never know your reasons for needing a trophy boy, so let's call this a relationship of mutual convenience and try to have some fun."

Mary's face flushes. "I just thought . . . ."

Paulie takes a deep breath. "Look, Mary, I don't want to be mean. It doesn't look good on me and it doesn't feel good. But I'm tapped out for being a nice guy right now."

Mary sits back. "Okay, I get that. So what do we do?"

"You bowl?" he asks.

"He told you to fuck off? Wow, that doesn't sound like Paulie." Arney grips the wheel and pushes back against the seat, pressing down on the accelerator.

"He was pissed," Hannah says. "No more pissed than I was."

"Did you tell him how you knew who it was?"

"Not really, I just told him it wasn't who *he* thought it was."

Arney says, "Maybe I shouldn't have told you. I didn't mean to pour gas on the fire. You and Paulie were great. Half the guys I know wished they had a girlfriend like you."

"You *should* have told me. Like I said, the one thing I can't stand is to be lied to. And leaving stuff out is the same as lying."

"Lying by omission."

"Exactly. I don't care what kind of a cool guy everyone thinks Paulie is, if he can't be true to his word, I can't be with him."

"I know you're right," Arney says, "and no matter how cool he is, it isn't cool to do that to the girl you're with." He's quiet a moment, gazing out the windshield at the countryside moving rapidly past as they speed along the two-lane road miles outside of town. "He's pretty pissed at me for hanging out with you now."

"He should have thought about that."

"Actually I told him that, not quite in those words. Guys who cheat always go with the impulse and then try to fix it. He should know that from watching his old man. Personally, I figured out a long time ago that bell is hard to un-ring."

"Well, you and I have no strings."

"Not for you, maybe," Arney says. "But for me. I'm not like the Bomb, I can't focus on more than one person. And that's okay. I get it that we're not a 'couple.' I just value loyalty above all else. I can't do it any other way."

"Arney, I'm not getting into anything."

"Understood," Arney says. "I know where you stand and I want you to know where I stand."

A mother quail and several chicks dash onto the road, sense Arney's car speeding toward them. Hannah tenses, looks at Arney, who doesn't brake and maybe even accelerates a bit. In the side-view mirror one of the chicks flaps on the pavement while another lies still and squashed.

Hannah stares at him in horror, thinks she sees the hint of a smile cross his lips, but instantly he says, "Damn! I thought they were going the other way! I thought I could speed up and get around them. Oh, God. That was awful!"

Hannah sits back, stunned, not sure what she just witnessed.

"We better go back," he says. "See if there's anything I can do."

"They're birds, Arney. They're dead."

"I can't believe I missed that," he says. "They ran out and I thought they'd go back. Jesus, I turned right into them." He is visibly upset.

Hannah takes a deep breath. "Just drive," she says finally. "We'll get over it. Let's just get to your parents' cabin and forget it."

.13

Arney Stack parks outside the Comfort Inn, leaves the car running, slings his backpack over his shoulder, and enters the front office. The girl behind the counter looks up and smiles, calls out, "Rick!" and continues reading *People*. Rick Praeger, a thin, dark-haired, handsome man in his early forties, wearing khakis and a knit polo shirt, emerges from the back office with a padded manila envelope and hands it to Arney.

Arney feels its weight, peeks inside, counts without removing any bills. "This isn't right," he says.

"Woody says there's a note," Rick says.

"About what?"

Praeger's hands go up. "Just the messenger."

Arney drives two blocks to a vacant lot. He pulls in, leaving the engine running, and opens the envelope. He dumps out the contents. There is cash—considerably less than Arney anticipated—and a short note: "Arney, you are a master at what you do and your contribution to our investment is invaluable. We couldn't have found a better colleague. Your insight on this project has been uncanny. Unfortunately your part of the return on our investment hasn't panned out this week. When you overachieve you are compensated. When you underachieve . . . well, John says that's why it's called a high-risk investment. With the remedy to this situation will come full restitution of agreed-upon monies." The note is unsigned.

Arney slams the heels of his hands against the wheel. "Those *bitches!*" He sits a moment to calm himself, but an almost murderous rage burns inside. "And fuck John. This operation doesn't exist without me!" He slams the wheel several more times. "Who's taking all the fucking risks?" He accelerates onto the street.

Paulie marches up the walk to the Wells mansion. *What am I doing?* He thinks. *Logs is right. I should steer clear of this.*

"Hi, Paulie. She's not here." Becca, Mary's younger

sister by three years, stands in the doorway.

"Really," Paulie says, though he's actually relieved. "She said I should pick her up at six-thirty." He glances at his watch.

"I don't think she came home from school," Becca says. I got here a little bit late, but I haven't seen her."

"Your parents here?"

Becca nods toward the house. "Mom's at her exercise group." Her voice lowers. "But the King is here. And he's *mad*." She steps onto the porch and in almost a whisper, says, "How did you get him to let you hang out with her?"

Paulie smiles. "Persistence, I guess."

"Persistence around here would get most guys killed. You know Roddy Blackburn?"

Paulie nods. "Yeah, I know Roddy."

"Well, tell him your secret."

"Becca, your dad may be a hardass, but I know *hippie* parents that wouldn't let their daughters go out with Roddy Blackburn. That kid was voted 'Most Likely to Take a Life.'"

She looks back toward the door again, lowering her voice even more. "He's a bandit, all right, but *God*."

Paulie turns back toward his car. "Tell Mary to give me a

call when she gets back," he says. "If, you know, she isn't chained to her bed." He looks into the garage. The Lexus is missing.

In Period 8 the following day, Mary Wells's seat is empty.

The quacking of a duck emanates from Paulie's front pocket, and he extracts his iPhone to see a message from Justin.

meet me. impt.

where?

u pik

rocket

10

Paulie enters through the back, passes Justin and Josh Takeuchi carrying two cinnamon rolls apiece and a large fruit smoothie. He smiles. "One of those for me?"

"*Might* be for you," Justin says, "but I'm gonna eat it."

Tak smiles and pats his stomach. "Still operating in the minus," he says.

Paulie steps behind the counter, pours himself a black coffee, and snags a piece of coffee cake. He joins Justin and Tak at the corner table in the back.

"What's goin' on?"

Justin takes a bite out of the first roll and a swig of his

smoothie. "Went around Diamond Lake to Twisted Crick last night with some brothers," he says and nods at Josh. "And Tak. Over to that spot where the Thumpers go on Fridays. Smoke some weed and get ready for finals."

"Different kind of study group," Paulie says. "What are you doing hanging out with these criminals, Tak?"

"You know, just gettin' all UNICEF with 'em," Tak says.

"Anyway, Arney came by with your honey and some other folks—"

"My ex-honey."

"Yeah, her. We're all getting baked, somebody brought some brew, and we just get talkin' about shit."

"Out to destroy the academic curve?" Paulie says.

"Yeah, we didn't do a lot of studyin' but Stack gets loose, starts talkin' about chicks who got no core."

"No *core*?"

"You know," Tak says, "nothin' to 'em. They just do what they have to, to keep going. To keep people liking 'em."

"Some of the girls get pissed," Justin says, "start callin' him, like, a bigot."

"That doesn't sound like Arney," Paulie says. "He can be a dick, but he usually keeps his ugliest thoughts under wraps and gets all cheesy about making people's lives better."

"Yeah, but we know how much bullshit that is. Always has been."

"Yeah."

"When you get fucked up like that, you don't change into another person, just tell truths you don't usually tell, right?" Justin says. "So Hannah's startin' to *seethe* and Stack says, 'You could get yours back, if you'd get the guts to really leave Paulie Bomb in the dust. You know, walk the walk.' Man, Murph about comes across the fire at him, but he backs up and says he was messin' with her. Then he starts throwin' out names—names of girls who weren't there."

"Like . . ."

"Girl that was cryin' in P-8 the other day," Justin says.

"Kylie."

"Yeah, her. And the Virgin Mary."

"Hey man, we're not callin' her that anymore."

"Mary, then. Anyway, Stack says this time he thinks she's gone for good."

"What?"

"Says there's no *insides* to her. Girl like that'll do anything, he says. Said last time he thought she was just havin' a freak-out, but he's takin' bets she's down the road for good."

"How the hell would he know that? She told me she hates his guts. No way she's telling him anything personal. He was messed up, right? Bein' all knowledgeable and shit like he does?"

Tak says, "Yeah but this was *freaky*. So freaky Hannah rides home with Jus and me."

Justin nods. "By the time we got her home she was pissed past *reason*. Said she never should'a spent one second with him, that she was just pissed at you."

Paulie sits back. "Gotta be careful what you do when you're pissed. It can bite you later." He laughs. "Besides, Hannah should know I do more damage being pissed at myself than she could ever do." He takes a bite of the coffee cake, washes it down. "Hmm. So maybe I'm not 'in the dust'?"

Justin raises his eyebrows.

"What else did Hannah say?" Paulie asks.

"Nothin' important." Justin looks straight at him. "You're not done with that girl, are you?"

Paulie smiles. "Maybe they'd been talking about me. Maybe that's why she was so pissed."

Justin nods. "I wouldn't get too cocky," he says. "The

way Stack was talkin' she would have been pissed if she never met you." He smiles. "But it could take a turn."

"I won't hold my breath," Paulie says, though he *would*. "But I'm worried about Mary. I was kind of relieved when I went to pick her up and she wasn't home. I thought she'd at least tell me if things went haywire again. Her sister was there and I *think* her parents, but the house was dark last night when I drove by, so I'm hoping she came back and they all went somewhere. It would make sense that her dad would get her away from here."

"That'd be nice, but I'm telling you bro, there was something *wrong* with the way Stack was talkin'. *He* sure didn't think she was off somewhere with her parents. He *knew* some shit."

Tak stands. "Man, I gotta get going and this man is my ride." He punches Justin's shoulder.

"This shit is crazy," Justin says, shaking his head as he follows Tak out.

Paulie grabs a refill and digs into his backpack, dragging out his dog-eared copy of *The Lone Ranger and Tonto Fistfight in Heaven*. As good a book as it is, his mind keeps drifting back to Hannah, hard as he works to keep that from happening. A half hour passes before he feels the quick vibration of a text.

It says, *soryigot uontothis mitenotgetvack wouldsaymorbut beter udon't no imstar danger watoverhead to manymistakesto*

It stops mid-sentence.

Paulie goes cold. He looks quickly at the keyboard on his iPhone. *Sory...sorry I got you onto this* . . . into *this*. It takes almost a minute to make *mitenotgetvack* into *might not get back*. *Imstar* makes no sense however he looks at it. There is only a number—no name—but it has to be Mary. The only person in his life that got him into anything, besides himself, is Mary.

He punches in the number but it goes straight to the message center, which informs him that the Verizon customer does not answer. It does not take messages.

He punches Mary's regular cell, leaving a message to "Call me," then gets no answer on Logs's cell or the Wells's home number.

His mind scrambles, then he punches the keyboard again, puts the cell to his ear. "Dad?"

"Ah," his father says on the other end, "my spawn. What's up?"

"Buy you dinner. Gotta run something past you."

"An offer I can't refuse," his dad says. "I took my car to get serviced this morning and didn't get off in time to pick it up, so you'll have to drop by and get me."

"On my way," Paulie says.

"What, no IHOP?" his father says as Paulie pulls into the parking lot at Two-7, a local sports bar with a varied menu. "What's the occasion?"

"Getting you some culture," Paulie says.

They sit in the family section and order. The waiter brings a Coke and a microbrew, gives them time to go over the menu.

"So what's going on?"

He shows his father Mary's text and translates it.

"Wow."

"What do I do?"

"You call her parents."

"I did. No answer."

His dad stares at the message. "I wouldn't know where to go with this," he says. "No answer. You think maybe her parents are forcing her into rehab?"

"I don't think so. But she disappeared before. Isn't it all strange enough to—"

"Tell you what, let's run by their place and look for lights. If her parents are home and Mary's not, they can decide what to do. Victor Wells has enough mojo to get the cops looking again."

They wolf down their meals while Paulie tells his dad everything he knows and most of what he's afraid of, then take the long way back to the hotel, past the darkened Wells mansion. "Nobody home," Paulie's dad says. "Do they have a vacation home? Can't believe a guy with his kind of dough wouldn't. I wish the text had said more, 'kidnapped by my parents' or something."

Paulie drives back to the hotel parking lot, a sinking feeling engulfing him. "Dad, Mary flips around a lot, like from pretty sane to really crazy, but she wouldn't send a message like that unless something was really wrong."

"You say you don't think it's rehab but anyone who gets on oxys once can get sucked back in," his father says. "You said yourself this girl is a completely different kid than you've known. Let's not overreact. I'm willing to bet this clears itself up by tomorrow. Statistically the worst-case scenario doesn't usually play out, you know that. I'm betting you hear from her again soon and all this will make sense. But you call me if you think I can help."

Paulie brakes in front of his dad's room. "Thanks, Dad." He leans over and gives him a quick, uncomfortable hug. "By the way, what's the latest on your imminent return?"

"Not so imminent," his dad says. "I think maybe you were right: your mom's had enough. I'm moving out of here in a week and getting into something semi-permanent."

Paulie watches him get out of the car, rolls down the window as he closes the door. "Whatever happens," he says, "you're still my dad. I just want you guys to stop killing each other."

Roger Baum grimaces. "And you," he says. "Listen, you let the so-called adults handle this. Your mother promised she'd quit running her grief past you and I'll make sure none of it lands on you from my end, okay? You just get your ass out of school and on to the next thing. Mary will turn up."

Paulie nods.

"And one more thing. Whatever happened with Hannah, happened. It doesn't mean you're like me, okay? I love your mom, and she loves me, but we never should have gotten married. If I'd had *any* foresight, I'd have known my weaknesses would take us down. You don't have those weaknesses. I sometimes wonder if you're really my kid."

Paulie nods again. "Thanks, Dad. Love you."

"Back atcha. And by the way, you're the reason whatever our marriage has turned into was worth it."

"Jesus Christ." Logs stands in his doorway in his sweats at 10 PM staring at the text on Paulie's iPhone.

"Yeah."

"Have you showed this to anyone else?"

"My dad. His thinks it's family related, that the cops wouldn't do anything without the parents reporting it."

"Mary has never had a flair for the dramatic, that *I* know of," Logs says, reading the text again. "No offense to your dad, but I'd rather err on the side of caution. We need someone else's eyes on this. First thing in the morning I'll get Wells's cell number from the front office and see if I can locate him. If Mary's with him, that's cool, but this doesn't feel right."

"I know. What scares me is, remember how Hannah said Mary was *on* something that night on the road? Mary told me it was oxys."

Logs grimaces. "That's a pretty addictive drug."

"She said she only used it once."

"There are drugs that would make a liar out of *you* and

oxycodone is one of them," Logs says, "but let's not jump to conclusions. What we have is a text from Mary Wells and the word 'danger.'"

"You think she's mixed up with drug guys?" Paulie says.

"Let me get dressed and we'll run down and do an FYI with the city cops, just to get it on the record."

"Cops just going to think we're, like, alarmists?"

"Probably, but what's to lose? More than likely the Wellses will come home and what we don't know now, we'll know then. I just hope Mary is with them."

.14

"Officer Rankin."

John Rankin stares at an unfamiliar face. "Do I know you?"

"Bruce Logsdon. I teach at the high school. We met at 'Dragnet in the Park.'"

"Ah, yes sir. What can I do for you?"

"The guy at the desk said you were the person to talk to about things 'Wells related.'"

"True," Rankin says. "Why, did something come up? I'm technically off duty. Strictly day shift. I was logging some overtime; catching up on paperwork."

"I know the feeling," Logs says. "This won't take long, and it'll probably seem frivolous, but my friend Mr. Baum here got a disturbing text message from the Wells girl, on the heels of her being absent again."

Rankin perks up. "Really?"

Logs nods at Paulie. "Show him."

Rankin takes his time reading the message. Paulie translates.

"I understand this doesn't rise to the level that would bring action by you guys," Logs says, "but it seemed like a good idea to get it on the record in case it turns into something."

"Good idea," Rankin says. "Do me a favor and forward it to my cell and I'll write it down when I get a chance." He gives Paulie his number. "You were smart to bring it."

They're walking back toward the car when Officer Rankin hollers, "Wait."

They turn in unison.

"It's probably a good idea to keep the text to yourself," Rankin says. "I mean, don't even tell your friends for now, Paulie. I doubt there's been foul play—there seems to be a lot of parent-child conflict in that house—but on the off chance that this turns into evidence, the fewer people know about it the better." He smiles. "One of those 'pieces of information not generally known.' You good with that?"

"It makes sense," Logs says. He turns to Paulie. "You keep this between us?"

"Sure," Paulie says. "No sweat."

"We've done what we can do," Logs says to Paulie as they get back into his car in front of the police station.

"Man," Paulie says, "Mary's dad has his own private police officer. Everything 'Wells related'?"

"Small town, big money I guess," Logs says.

Frank's Diner is a block ahead. "You wanna grab something real quick?" Logs asks.

They pull into the nearly empty parking lot and sit a moment.

"My crazy brain is telling me one thing," Paulie says.

"What's that?"

"Arney Stack is in this somehow."

Logs motions for them to go inside. "How so?"

They walk in and sit at the deserted counter. A young man, probably college age, runs a wet rag over it. Dim light reveals an empty room. Both order shakes; chocolate for Paulie, vanilla for Logs.

"Three different times lately he's given me bullshit, like exactly opposite of what's true when there was no reason for it. Like he was lying just to see if he could.

When I caught him he gave me more bullshit."

Paulie tells Logs about his conversation with Justin earlier in the day, then about how he'd asked Arney to take Mary home the night of his big screwup—no pun intended—and how Arney lied about going to meet the Thumpers. "Either he was going someplace he didn't want me to know about or he was, like, setting me up with Mary for some stupid reason, and that *seriously* doesn't make sense. He'd said he was spending time with her, but then he gives me some crap excuse why he can't take her home."

Logs frowns.

"I know Mary isn't telling me everything," Paulie says. "I've tried to call her on it, but she just plays dumb. She's like this hurt little kid one minute and then like a . . . I don't know, a fucking *vampire*. And I ain't talking *Twilight*. I don't know. It's *crazy;* there's no *reason* for anything."

"Or one you don't see."

"Yeah, that. And fucking Stack has his hand in everything. He tells me it was Hannah's idea to start hanging out with him. I can't prove it, but no fucking way. That's not Hannah. She might rub my face in it, letting me see her with him if he went to her, but no way she sets it up."

The shakes are placed in front of them. "Thanks,

man," Paulie says to the kid behind the counter. "I could drink five of these a day," he says to Logs.

Logs lays his straw on the counter and drinks directly from the glass. "Keep going."

"Okay. Back when Mary first 'went missing,' Arney tells us he knows Mary better than anyone, that she'll be back and okay, wouldn't screw up her scholarship. When I asked *her* if she has any kind of relationship with him, she says, 'Yeah, I hate his guts.' Doesn't go into it, like every other goddamn thing. He tells us Mary's old man is a cool guy if you just get to know him—not scared of him at all. Turns out Mr. Wells knows him as some community service partner for Mary. Period. I mean, why's Arney even bringing her up? Who gives a shit if he knows her better than the rest of us? He had to be wondering the same things we were wondering when she showed up missing." He takes a sip of his shake. "I guess you can't *show up* missing, but you know what I mean."

"I do."

"*Then,*" says Paulie, "according to Justin and Tak, he and Hannah show up on the other side of Diamond Lake, where Justin and some of his crew were smok—studying, and goes into this rant about girls with no *core*. Even takes a shot at Hannah. Gets so nasty, Hannah won't ride home with him. One of his 'no core' girls was Mary. Another one was Kylie."

"No core?" Logs says.

"Yeah, like they need somebody else to tell them who they are."

Logs sits a moment, considering. "What else?"

"I sure don't buy his plea for world peace in P-8. Gives us all that crap about his legacy as ASB prez. 'We gotta take care of each other.' Then he talks this shit about Mary and Kylie. Then there's his big business deal."

"I guess I don't know about that."

"Supposedly his old man gave him a bundle to *invest*. Hooked him up with some business guys downtown and bankrolled him big enough to make it worth their while. Arney says his dad wants him to know how to handle real money."

"You think *that's* related?"

"I don't know that *any* of this is related," Paulie says as they head back to the car. "I just know I have the same gut feeling about all of it. Shit, it's probably just the feeling I have about Arney since he started hanging out with Hannah."

Logs watches Paulie struggle with it. If all this is related, there are some really loose strings.

"Anyway," Paulie says, "stuff either makes sense or it doesn't, and since the night I cheated on Hannah, a hell of a lot more doesn't than does. I know I'm obsessed, so it's all running together, but . . . wanna hear something *really* crazy?"

Logs laughs. "Don't stop now."

"I was looking back on the night I messed up, when Mary asked me to dance."

"And . . ."

"I swear, there was this look on Arney's face when she asked me. It was like he sicced her on me. Then the day you and I saw her up at the lake; that day she came back, she said there were things she couldn't tell me. 'Awful things,' she said. I thought she was talking about her dad, but now I'm not so sure. Arney . . ."

"You think Arney is actually involved in Mary's disappearance."

"Couldn't be, right?" Paulie says. "He's a fucking kid, like me."

"I think you're probably pissed at him, Paulie, but some of this stuff is easy to check out," Logs says. "Tomorrow I'll see if I can track Mr. Wells down and find out if he knows where Mary is. We'll go from there. Until then, there's nothing to do if you don't get more messages from Mary, so why don't you go home and try to get some sleep."

"Because I have to go home and get at least one paragraph down on my senior thesis, or I'm going to be stuck in this hellhole without you."

Logs puts his hand on Paulie's head. "Go forth and write as if your life depended on it, grasshopper, because it does. I'll catch up with you tomorrow."

Draft V

What do you do when you know your brain isn't developed enough to do the right thing? Brain scientists tell us the adolescent brain isn't quite "cooked" yet. The evolution of the individual follows the pattern of the evolution of the species. The emotional brain—the instinctive brain—has been fully evolved in those species in line to turn into humans for millions of years. The rational brain—evident only in humans—has been evolved for, in relative terms, a blink of an eye. (Medina; Brain Rules). The development of the individual brain follows that same pattern. The emotional aspect is fully formed at an early age, but the rational aspect doesn't become fully developed until the early to mid-twenties (Medina; Brain Rules). Which accounts for why teenagers often do what seems like some spectacularly stupid shit.

But to say that the rational brain isn't fully developed in adolescence isn't to say that it isn't almost there. The more we know about where that development is headed, the better chance we have of making better, more adultlike decisions.

(Okay, that's further than I've gotten before. Taking my partially developed brain to bed.)

Paulie hits the light and lays his head back on his pillow, staring out his bedroom window at a starry, moonless night, imagining being Bruce Logsdon on that day toward the end of 1968 when he first saw a photograph of our blue ball hanging in the void of space, and all that couldn't be seen from that distance. His mind drifts toward semiconsciousness when suddenly Mary's face flashes before him. What if she's out there in some tortuous situation and can't call for help? What if her last text ever was to his phone? Was she suicidal? "Might not make it back" could mean a lot of things. *sory I got u into this.* What? What did she get him into? And what is the danger? His imagination is driving him crazy. The one person he'd give anything to talk to has nothing for him but contempt. Truth be told, as angry and hurt and disappointed as *he's* been, he'd do anything to make up with her.

• • •

Logs rolls into the school parking lot an hour early and lets himself into the main office, determined to clear up as much of the Mary Wells mystery as he can. He brings up the Wellses' numbers on the office computer: home and cells for Mom, Dad, and Mary, noticing that Mary's number does not correspond to the one that popped up on Paulie's phone last night. He slips a note under Dr. Johannsen's door: *Please call my room ASAP. Logs*

He walks through the breezeway, into the math/science department foyer and toward his room, lost in thought.

"Hey, Mr. Logs."

He looks up to see Hannah Murphy on the carpeted hallway floor next to his door, writing in a notebook and texting.

"Hannah. *You're* early."

"You have no idea."

"Been here awhile, huh?" Logs glances around the empty foyer. "How'd you get in?"

"Mr. Branson was just finishing up in your office."

"Well, since you're sitting next to *my* door, I'm guessing you want to talk with *me*."

"This is why you're my favorite teacher. You're so *smart*."

Logs unlocks his door and they go inside. "What can I do for you?"

"Mr. Logs, I think I might have made a big mistake."

"Tell me."

"With Paulie."

Logs's eyebrows go up involuntarily.

"You think so, too."

"Look, Hannah, I love you both, I do. And I'll be honest: I used to think there weren't two kids more perfect for each other. But life ain't predictable and things happen. We all have to figure out how to negotiate them."

"I was being a bitch hanging out with Arney."

"Your words, but I know."

"I can't tell you how stupid that was."

Logs smiles. "You don't have to."

Hannah takes a deep breath. "Actually that's not why I'm here—the stuff with me and Paulie, I mean. I can deal with that."

Logs waits.

"It's Arney."

"What about him?"

"I told him I'd go out to his family cabin last weekend to help get it ready for summer. I thought it would be nice to just get away, and he and I had been getting along okay. Like friends." She looks at her feet. "And I guess I wanted Paulie to think we went there for a different reason."

Logs's face is expressionless. It's not his job to judge, but he's had a trace of ill will toward Hannah for choosing Arney of all people to rub Paulie's nose in. Not that Paulie didn't have it coming. . . .

"I know, I know. Like I said, I was being a bitch. At any rate, Arney seemed cool enough, but he was saying things about Paulie that couldn't be true."

"Such as."

"Mr. Logs, something's seriously wrong with Arney."

"Did he get out of line?"

Hannah laughs. "You think there has to be something wrong with a guy to make a move on me?"

"I meant . . ."

"I know. Yeah, he made a move, but I expected that and it wasn't going to happen. But we had a few beers and he got into this fancy scotch his dad keeps hidden up there, and he said some things . . . he was like, *hateful*."

"Mel Gibson Syndrome. Get plastered and out comes the real you."

She tells Logs about the birds following their mother

across the two-lane. "He swerved right into them," she says. "It was creepy. I looked at his face and he was . . . I don't know, proud, or smug or something. Then when he saw how horrified I was he blurted out this stupid story about how he thought they were going to reverse direction, but Mr. Logs, they *couldn't* have. They were full-speed ahead trying to get out of the way. I didn't think it was so weird right then because I wanted to believe him, I guess."

"And that was before he was drinking?"

"Only coffee," she says. "We were on our way *up.*"

"That's troubling."

"On the way home we stop by to see Justin and some other kids and he goes *way* off, calling people—girls—horrible names and saying things . . . worse than earlier. He even started going after *me*. Justin took me home." She breathes deep. "How in the world did we elect him student body president?"

Two sharp knocks. "Hey, man . . ." Paulie stops cold. "Hey, Hannah."

"Hey, Paulie."

Logs watches them lock eyes. Hannah blinks first. "Paulie, I'm sorry about the other day in The Rocket."

"I shouldn't have said that," Paulie says. "You know me,

when things start to go bad I gotta speed them up."

Logs winces.

"I probably had it coming," Hannah says.

Paulie studies her a moment. "Well, this is awkward," he says finally. "I'll leave you two to your sordid affair."

"Actually we were finished with that," Logs says. "Pull up a chair." He holds up a slip of paper. "Got the numbers we needed. Thought I'd give Mr. Wells a little time to wake up."

Hannah crinkles her nose. "What's going on?"

"Mary Wells seems to be AWOL again," Logs says. "We're trying to find out if she's with her family."

"Doesn't Mrs. Byers take care of that?"

Logs nods at Paulie as if to say, "Bring her up to speed," while he punches Victor Wells's cell number.

While Paulie shows her the text message on his own cell, Logs speaks into his.

"Mr. Wells? This is Bruce Logsdon . . . from the high school? I'm calling in reference to Mary's attendance. Is your family out of town? . . . You and your wife are? Becca. Not Mary? . . . I'm afraid so . . . Two days; we're a little worried. Paul Baum got a text from her, or a partial text. . . ."

He listens for what seems to Paulie like a long time, then,

"I wouldn't jump to conclusions . . . I know, she's not my daughter . . . Yes, sir. This afternoon, then? Sure, I'll stay 'til you get here. And I'll call if she shows this morning . . . Please let us know if you hear from her. Yes, sir, thank you."

"She's not with him," Logs says. "There was an emergency in Mrs. Wells's family. Mary stayed home to catch up on some work. He didn't know she hadn't been to school." He shakes his head. "My God, Wells is pissed at her for causing him more problems. I'd be worried out of my head. Hell, now I *am* worried out of my head." He slaps his hand flat on his desktop. "Listen, I'm going over to the office to talk with Dr. Johannsen; I'll catch up with you in P-8." And he is out the door.

"I can't believe her dad left her alone," Hannah says. She hesitates. "You think she's back on whatever she was on the night I almost ran her over?"

"Oxys," Paulie says. "I don't think so; that freaked her out pretty bad." He shakes his head. "But like Logs says, bring in drugs and all bets are off."

Hannah moves closer, sits on the edge of the desk next to Paulie's chair. He aches to reach out to touch her. It almost seems she would let him.

"So this is more than just Mary Wells getting into drugs?" she asks.

He nods. "It sure seems like it."

Hannah touches his hand.

"Hey," he says in barely a whisper. "Truce?"

"Yeah," Hannah says. "For now."

"In case your day's starting slow, Mary Wells is missing again."

"My God," Dr. Johannsen says, sitting back in her chair. "Where did you hear that? Her father again?"

"Actually I told *him*," Logs says. "Paulie had been hanging out with her right before she disappeared, and got a strange text message, one that worried him. He and his dad drove over, found no one home, and because of all the recent uproar, he came to me. I caught up with Mr. Wells this morning. He's out of town with his wife and younger daughter, but Mary was supposed to stay home to catch up on all the work she missed. He's coming back this afternoon. I thought you and I could meet with him."

"Goodness, yes," Dr. Johannsen says. "Let's head this one off and see if we can get this year over without my having to stand in front of one more camera."

Rachel Randolph, the front office receptionist and secretary, rushes into the office.

"What is it, Rachel?"

Rachel's face radiates alarm. "Come look."

Logs and Dr. Johannsen step into the empty outer office and see the TV monitor mounted above the entrance door, tuned to the local news. Police tape surrounds a modest house, still smoldering from what must have been an intense fire. Police cars, lights flashing, sit at the edge of the lawn and firemen roll in their hoses.

Logs can't place the house, but the neighborhood looks vaguely familiar. "What is this?"

"Kylie Clinton's house," Rachel says. "She's one of our students."

Logs's stomach leaps into his throat. He didn't see her after her meltdown in Period 8. *She said she was okay.* He leans forward on the counter. "What are they saying? Was anyone hurt?" The video is obviously from last night. A girl with her face intentionally blurred is helped into the back of an ambulance by paramedics and a woman who must be her mother. The woman gets in behind her.

"The fire chief says there's a gasoline smell everywhere," Rachel says. "He didn't come out and say it was arson because they have to do a formal investigation, but . . ."

"She had her hands over her face," Logs says. "Do you think they blurred it because she was burned?"

"I don't think so," Dr. Johannsen says. "She would have been on a stretcher. They blurred it because she's a juvenile."

Logs hits his forehead. "Duh!"

They watch the scenario play out repeatedly, but no new information comes to light. "I will be *so* glad when this school year is over," Dr. Johannsen says. "I swear I feel responsible for everything that happens to these kids nine months out of the year, whether the school has anything to do with it or not."

Logs stares at the screen. The images aren't live. *If Kylie isn't burned, what's she doing getting into an ambulance?*

.15

Dr. Johannsen walks onto the stage in a stone-silent auditorium, the counselors and other administrators in folding chairs next to the podium. Justin and Tak sit between Paulie and Hannah near the front.

Dr. Johannsen taps the mike with her finger. "Good morning, people. For those of you who don't know, the family of one of our students experienced a major house fire last night. A few minutes ago I got off the phone with someone from the city fire department, who says there is evidence of foul play, which I assume means arson. They've requested to come into the school today to ask questions of anyone who might be able to shed light on their investigation. Your teachers will bring you up to date on the details, and we'd like anyone who thinks they might have *any* useful information to excuse yourself to the office. *Please* do not use it as simply an excuse to get yourself out of class."

Light laughter.

"Okay," Dr. Johannsen says, "return to your first period and let's see if we can do this in a fashion that doesn't cause too much interruption in the day."

The mass exodus begins.

"I saw on TV that a neighbor said Kylie was yelling it was her fault," Justin says.

"Kylie *or* her mom," Hannah says.

"Yeah, well," Tak says, "what's your bet? Remember her in P-8 the other day?"

The others don't respond. They remember.

"Second news report said no one was injured," Paulie says. "So what's with the ambulance?"

Justin smiles. "Two kinds of hospital you go to in an ambulance," he says.

Paulie and Hannah say it together: "Psych ward."

"So," Paulie says, gazing at Justin and Tak, "Sixty-four-thousand-dollar question. Where the hell is Mary Wells?"

"I guess that used to be a lot of money, huh?" Justin says.

Tak says, "Yeah, back when they made up the saying. Mr. Logs was probably younger than us."

"I caught up with him on the way out of school," Paulie says. "He's still gonna meet up with her dad this afternoon. He said he'd call if he learns anything."

"Lot of *crazy* shit happenin' around here," Justin says.

"A *lot of crazy shit.*" Tak agrees. He sips his hot chocolate. "What do you guys think about Kylie? House is on fire and she's yellin' it's her fault?"

"That neighbor wasn't sure who was yelling," Paulie says. "And you know the news guys, they'll say anything to get some suspense going."

"Maybe," Justin says, "but she gets all freaky the other day in P-8. Might make sense she's freaky when the ol' home catches fire."

Paulie rocks his chair back on two legs, staring at the screen on his cell. "I was gonna hit the water this afternoon, but I'm afraid I might miss something."

Justin says, "I just want to hear what Wells is gonna say. Shit, man, his daughter is missing and he's more pissed and embarrassed than freaked. What a sorry . . ."

• • •

Paulie enters Period 8 late the next day, sees an open seat next to Hannah and slips into it.

Logs says, "So, who wants to start?"

"How about you start, Mr. Logs," Marley Waits says. "You know any more about Mary? And what about Kylie?"

"This is probably confidential," he says, "but we keep it all in the room, right?"

"Yeah, man," Justin says. "We keep it in the room."

"They took Kylie to the psychiatric unit."

Taylor Max says, "She start the fire?"

"No, Taylor, she didn't start the fire. She got hysterical and they couldn't calm her down. She's there for a seventy-two-hour observation. That's about all I can tell you."

"Was the neighbor lady right?" Bobby Wright asks. "Was she yelling that it was her fault?"

"I have no idea," Logs says, "and how about we keep the conjecture to a minimum. Maybe when all of this calms down she can tell us herself."

"So what about Mary?" Marley asks.

"I don't know a thing. I was supposed to meet with her father yesterday afternoon, but he didn't show up. Either he didn't get back or he decided not to keep us in the loop. I'm sure he's contacted the police."

"Jesus Christ," Hannah says. "Your kid is missing and you take a couple of days to come home?"

"I got the feeling on the phone that Mr. Wells thinks Mary took off to cause trouble for him," Logs says. "Since she disappeared that first time, he isn't giving her much slack."

"God," Marley says. "Do we know her better than her own dad?"

"Doesn't sound like that would be much of an achievement," Tak says.

Arney bursts through the door. "Hey, everybody. Sorry I'm late. Student council meeting."

"Emergency meeting to save the school?" Justin says.

Arney ignores the sarcasm. "Something like that." He doesn't make eye contact with Paulie or Hannah. Or Justin, for that matter. To the rest of the room he says, "We set up a plan to gather donations for the Clintons, and to send a card up to Kylie." He looks directly at Logs. "Man, I missed that one. I thought she was okay after I talked with her the other day."

Logs only nods.

Hannah leans over to Paulie. "Arney's so full of shit. You should have heard him talking about her the other night."

"Don't tell me," Paulie says. "Tell him."

Hannah stares at Paulie a second, then looks over to Arney. "Why would you be involved in sending her a card after all those things you said about her the other night?"

Arney shakes his head, looks at his hands. "I meant to talk to you in private," he says, "and to you guys, too, Jus. I was way out of line. I think I'm one of those guys who needs to stay clean and sober every minute. I talked to my dad this morning and he's looking into getting me into a program."

"Really," Hannah says. "Which one?"

Arney doesn't miss a beat. "Daybreak, probably," he says. "Outpatient."

Justin leans over to Paulie. "That fucker is *slick*."

Hannah smiles. *It's always something you can't check with Arney,* she thinks. *Daybreak is confidential. He can say anything he wants. I'll bet anything he knows at least three kids' names who go there, and he'll drop them on us within the week. Swear to God if I didn't know better I'd think he had something to do with Kylie going off. Mary, too.*

Paulie leans toward her. "I wish you'd have let me talk," he whispers, "about the thing with Mary." He hesitates. "It wasn't exactly what it looked like."

Hannah grits her teeth, then slides down in her seat.

"You're right," he says, "It is what it is. But I like the truce." He reaches over, drums his fingers on her knee.

She covers his hand with hers.

"Keep the truce?"

She nods tentatively, glances over at Arney, who is watching, then away.

"It's good to get back into a pattern," Logs says to Paulie. Hannah drives toward them, her scull mounted atop her car.

"And good to have her back," Paulie says. "I'm glad she didn't make us wait 'til she got her new boat."

"Be patient, my friend," Logs says in a low voice as Hannah gets out of the car.

They help Hannah get the scull into the water. "Thanks for coming," Logs says. He looks out over the water, then at the sun low in the sky. "We don't have a lot of light, so what say you guide us out a little over halfway, then we'll hook on and you can pull us back. We'll all get a quick workout, then come earlier next time and do some real work. We're getting a little more light every day."

They launch the boat off the end of the loading dock. Paulie and Logs slide into the water.

On the seat of his Beetle, Paulie's iPhone vibrates with an incoming text.

Paulie and Logs speed toward the city police station in Logs's pickup, Paulie staring at the text and Logs breaking nearly every traffic law that won't get them killed, hoping to get pulled over for speeding, thereby picking up an escort.

When Paulie saw the text just after they shed their wetsuits, he panicked. He praises the gods that Logs was there—Logs, who seems to *never* panic. Hannah read the message and headed for Mary's house, leaving the scull on the dock, dialing and re-dialing the number Logs gave her for Mr. Wells's cell on the way.

"If he answers tell him or his wife to meet us at the station," Logs had told her. "If he doesn't and he's not home, leave a note. *Make* him understand how urgent it is."

"I'd have you call 911," Logs says to Paulie now, "but I don't know where to send them. Officer Rankin gave me his private cell and said to call any time if something related to Mary came up." He spits out Rankin's number from memory. "Don't know how I can do that," he says. "I can't remember to get cat food. If he answers tell him to meet us at the station."

Paulie is dialing as Logs says it; Rankin answers on the second ring. In as few words as possible Paulie relates the facts. "We're on our way to the station now," he says.

"I'll be there in fifteen," Rankin says. "Meet me outside. I can set things in motion faster than you could starting your story from scratch with the desk."

Logs floors the gas pedal of the old Datsun. They speed onto the off-ramp and onto city streets, running rapidly changing yellow lights at busy intersections and red lights at empty ones.

Officer Rankin waits as they pull into a no-parking zone in front of the station. "What have you got?"

Paulie punches "Messages" on his iPhone and turns the screen toward Rankin, and translates. *telkylieto run wachout4arne myparents2 getsisandrundanger 4 any1hooreadsthis.*

"Jesus," Rankin says.

Logs says, "What do you think it means?"

"I don't know. You're going to have to let me keep your phone this time, son," Rankin says. "I have a feeling this will be critical evidence."

Paulie reluctantly hands over the iPhone.

"So what do we do now?" Logs asks.

"Go home," Rankin says. "There's nothing you can do. If we need anything else we'll give a call." He takes Logs's numbers. "Again, don't give anyone the specific content of this." He holds up the phone. "And I mean no one."

"Man," Paulie says, sitting in the shotgun seat on the way back to the lake to retrieve his car and their gear. "Oh, man."

"What in the world could Mary know about Kylie?" Logs says. "Any way you look at it, this is *bad.*" He accelerates onto the freeway. "After we pick your stuff up, I'm following you home."

"Why?"

"To talk with your mom. We have no idea where Mary sent that text from, but it was *dire.* She said anyone who reads it is in danger and the message came to *your* phone." Logs moves into the right lane and onto the off-ramp. "I hope Hannah got in touch with the Wellses. If not, I'm sure Rankin will." He hands Paulie his cell. "Call her."

Paulie punches in Hannah's number while Logs takes a right onto the narrow two-lane that leads another mile and a half to the lake. Suddenly bright lights and an explosion of metal on metal rocket the pickup sideways and down the grassy incline. It rolls once before coming to a rest upright against a thick pine tree. Paulie and Logs sit stunned, steam and smoke pouring from under the hood, the horn blaring. Paulie's head clears, he checks for injuries, struggles with his seat belt.

"You okay? Paulie, you okay?"

"I think so. I can't see anything. Jesus, what happened?"

Logs slams the palm of his hand against the glove compartment, popping it open. He feels for the handle of a crescent wrench, finds it, and breaks out his side window, groping for the seat belt release. He knocks out the edges of the glass, peering up toward the road at headlights beaming above their heads. The driver's-side door of a dark SUV opens, casting a glow on the exiting driver, and a passenger following. In a split second it registers. "Run!" Logs shoulders his door, creating an opening just wide enough to slide out. "Paulie, run!"

"What? Where?"

"Get *out* of there!"

Paulie shoulders his door, but it's blocked by the trunk of a thick pine. "This side!" Logs's voice is low and tense. "Hurry!"

He pulls the driver's-side door open a hair farther and Paulie squeezes out. "Run!"

Paulie hasn't seen the two men moving down toward them through the waist-high grass and he starts to bolt toward the road. Logs hauls him back by his shirt collar. "Into the trees. Stay with me."

They move quickly, mostly by feel in the darkness, until Logs stops and they stand, listening. Logs puts a finger to his lips and pushes Paulie deeper into the trees, then stops again. The voices are distinctly farther away.

"What the hell is going on?"

"I don't know," Logs whispers, "but those guys rammed us on purpose."

"Jesus."

"Yeah, Jesus," Logs says. "The interior light came on when they got out . . . don't get freaked, but I think one of them is Rankin."

"Shit!"

"Yeah. And who*ever* it was meant to kill us. That vehicle was moving full speed."

"Man, you're scaring me."

"Good."

"What're we going to do?"

"We're going to get farther into these trees and give ourselves time to think. And *listen*. If their voices get closer, we gotta move."

"Shit, I quit Boy Scouts after a month. I can't tell which direction is which."

Logs points west. "Lake's that way." Then east. "Road's that way. We can't double back." As they stare toward the road, the horizon brightens, shadows grow more pronounced. "Sweet Jesus," he says, "more cars."

He puts a hand between Paulie's shoulders and moves him another twenty-five yards into the thickening forest.

"Logs, what *is* this?"

"I have a hunch, but *whatever* it is, we're in *way* over our heads. We need help." He slaps his head in realization. "Rankin has your cell and mine's in the truck."

"What's your hunch?"

"Just believe whoever's behind this has nothing to lose."

"What are we gonna *do*?"

Logs is silent, then, "We got one shot," he says.

Paulie gets it. "The lake."

Logs leads them over the forested hill toward Diamond Lake. Voices behind them fade, but light patterns in the trees tell them someone is on the move.

"This is going to be cold as hell," Logs whispers. "We can't go to your car or the dock. Rankin knows we were headed back there. We'll go north a couple hundred yards and get in through the tall grass."

"Then what?"

"I'm not sure. They'll probably check the shoreline. We might have to cross."

"The one thing we can do that they can't," Paulie says.

"There's no moon. It's easy to get disoriented in the dark. There are cabins on the other side, but they're back in the trees. We'll have to find *some* point to fix on."

Logs leads them well north of the dock. They emerge from the trees to see headlights back near Paulie's Beetle.

Paulie whispers, "Fuck."

"No, this is good," Logs says. "If they think we're dumb enough to go there, they'll have to leave someone. That means fewer guys to come looking. I don't have my glasses. Can you see how many?"

Paulie squints. "Three vehicles. Can't see how many guys."

"Too many, is how many." His voice drops even lower. "Now listen. We leave our clothes here. You still have your suit on, right?"

Paulie nods.

"Me, too. Everything else we bury. There are probably sticks and rocks and all kind of shit in the grass between here and the water. I don't care if you step on a rattlesnake, make *no* noise. Rankin is a cop. He's armed."

"Got it."

"That water's gonna be cold. When you hit it, you don't even suck air. Dead quiet. Hands and knees crawling in, breaststroke for at least five hundred yards. Sound carries, Paulie, and if they hear us, we're done."

"I'll do it. I'll do whatever."

Logs stares at him through the darkness. "I know you will. I'm just scared, just like you. We'll be fine."

They shed their clothes and quietly bury them beneath leaves and needles. The night air is cold and Paulie feels goose bumps rising. *This is nothing*, he thinks, *compared to what it's about to be.*

Logs stands, looking out at the blackness that is the lake. He points—a single dim light flickers on the other side. "There's our anchor point," he whispers.

Paulie squints. "It's the Thumpers," he says. "Friday nights, Firth and the other YFC kids go right where Twisted Crick runs into the lake. Build a big bonfire and sing songs and shit."

"Blessed be the Lord Jesus Christ," Logs says. He breathes deeply. "Okay, stick together. Breaststroke or sidestroke until I say different."

They crouch and move silently toward the water.

A powerful searchlight sweeps toward them; they simultaneously drop to their bellies in the tall grass. Logs watches as it passes over, then lifts his head, watches. "They're not sweeping the water. They haven't figured us out yet."

Paulie shakes uncontrollably. He can't feel the cold now, it's all fear.

When the light sweeps past again in the opposite direction, Logs says, "Let's do it."

.16

Hannah can't believe what she's hearing. "I'm washing my hands of that girl." Victor Wells stands facing her on the porch of the Wells mansion.

"You can't do that." Hannah clutches the scrap of paper onto which she copied the message from Paulie's phone.

"She put us through hell just a short time ago. She promised me this kind of situation was *finished*. I will *not* have her embarrassing this family again. Her mother is beside herself."

"But the text message says—"

"I don't care what it says. It's all lies with her recently. Why in the world would she contact Paul Baum instead of her own father?"

"Do you text, Mr. Wells? Do you? Do you have that function on your phone?" Hannah yells, glaring.

"Don't be silly. Of course I don't *text*. She knows my number, for crying out loud."

"Read the fucking message!" Hannah screams, and thrusts it to his chest. "She's in trouble! She can't call!"

Wells glances at the paper.

"Out loud," Hannah says. "Read it out loud. When this is over and they ask me if I told you what was going on, I want it known you understood."

Flushed bright red, Wells reads the message aloud, focusing, and softening a bit with each word. "My God, what is this?"

Hannah steps back. "I don't know. Mr. Logs and Paulie went to the police station. They tried to call you."

"Kylie. Who is that?"

"A girl from school. The girl whose house caught on fire."

"Why would my daughter be involved with a girl like that? I don't think Mary even knew her."

"She knew her! Believe the text! Believe she's in trouble! You should go somewhere."

"I have state-of-the-art security," Wells says, "and a healthy respect for the Second Amendment. We'll be fine.

Thanks for your concern, though, and . . . thanks for forcing me to pay attention. I'll call Officer Rankin right away."

"Okay. I'm gonna tell Mr. Logs to call you if he finds out anything, so answer your damn phone."

Wells nods. "Thank you again. I will."

He turns into the house. Hannah hears three clicks and four digital *beeps*. Floodlights bathe the lawn.

She steps into her car and calls Paulie. Two rings, then a click. She waits for his voice. "Paulie?"

A grunt.

"It's me, Hannah. Listen, I got to Mr. Wells. Jesus, what a hardass. Anyway, he's staying there. He says he has a first-rate security system. Probably snipers on the roof or something. He's going to call the police. Did you guys talk to the police? . . . Paulie?"

Call ended.

She tries again. Straight to voicemail.

She has only Logs's home number in her contacts so she punches that. Three rings, then: "You have reached . . . the end of your rope. Leave your call for help" *Beep*.

"You might be right, Mr. Logsdon. It's Hannah. Call me when you get this. I don't have your cell and I can't reach Paulie."

• • •

Standing next to the lime-green Beetle, Officer John Rankin takes Paulie's iPhone away from his ear and smiles. He moves quickly to his car radio, certain that Wells has called the station by now to see how the police are responding to Logs's disclosures. When the desk sergeant tells him yes, Mr. Wells called but he referred him to Rankin as he had been instructed, Rankin says, "Don't worry, I got it. I'll bring him in later and we'll get this all on paper."

Rankin crosses to the Audi parked on the other side of Paulie's Beetle, raps on the window. "Stack."

The window slides down halfway. "What do you know about this Hannah?"

"Used to be Bomb's girlfriend. I was using her to fuck with him a little. Thought I might be able to turn her, too, but she's too tough. She's my ace in the hole with Baum, though."

"Meaning?"

"When Woody kidnapped Mary instead of offing her, he fucked me good. My name's on that text. If we don't get Bomb and Mr. Logs, and if Woody doesn't grow some balls, I've gotta disappear. Hannah's gonna be my ticket."

"We'll all have to do that," Rankin says. "I've always known that day would come."

"Nice of you to let me know that," Arney says.

"Look, you psycho," Rankin says, "if you hadn't gone pyro on the Clinton place we might have some breathing room. I'm guessing she's keeping quiet. I scared her pretty good—but we can't get to her in the psych ward. So don't lay that on me. You've known you were on your own from the start."

Arney shrugs. "Whatever."

"Well, we've got one chance. The only people who've seen that text are the teacher and the Bomb kid, Hannah what's-her-name, and me. If we get them all, it'll be a while before this shit gets unraveled and we can disappear. If not, our pictures are going to be everywhere. I don't have to remind you what happens in prison to people like us."

"No," Arney says, "you do not."

Logs and Paulie slip into the water, holding their breath to keep from gasping from the frigid shock of it. They breaststroke, slowly at first, silent as eels. Every muscle tightens, groins ache as they wait for the warmth that comes with numbness. Logs curses their earlier training swim: they worked hard and neither has eaten. This will be done on a diet of adrenaline. They stroke, take measured breaths, increasing the distance between themselves and the lights at the dock. Logs taps Paulie's shoulder. "I can't see that far, but it looks like more cars. Am I right?"

Paulie rolls onto his back and peers toward the dock. "You're right," he whispers.

"Five more minutes and we swim for real," Logs says.

"Got it."

After only two, Logs taps him again, feeling urgent. The stress on his body is taking its toll. "Let's do it now. Stay together, we gotta listen for each other all the time. Keep the fire straight ahead of you. You're faster on the front end of these swims, but don't get too far ahead. We need two brains."

Paulie nods and they start their run. Grateful for their hundreds of hours in the water together, Paulie visualizes Logs's pace and falls into it. Every twenty strokes they breathe to the front, holding the growing firelight dead center. Bodies numb now, false warmth allows a quicker pace as muscles loosen and they pick up speed.

CRASH! Paulie involuntarily yells "Shit!" as his

head strikes the corner of an anchored ski float. Logs whirls in time to see the powerful searchlight sweeping toward them. He shoves Paulie's head down as he goes under himself, watching the surface from below as the light sweeps above them. He guides Paulie to the far side of the float.

"Fuck!" Paulie whispers. "Did they see us?"

"I don't know. Are you all right? Don't move." The light sweeps harmlessly back and forth while they hide behind the float.

"Wait," Logs says.

"Logs, man, we gotta keep movin'. We'll fuckin' freeze to death out here."

"*Wait,*" Logs says again.

The searchlight points back toward land and they start again, zoning in on the fire.

Paulie rolls over in time to see two cars pull out. He watches them speed down the dirt road leading around the lake. He catches Logs, taps his leg. "They're going around," he says.

"Damn! They heard us."

"Man, I'm sorry."

"It happened. Could just as easily have been me." They

tread, Logs's mind spinning and his energy draining. "If they go to the fire, we'll see them," he says finally. "The trees are about as far from the shore over there as they are on our side. If they show up there, we'll swim in to the north. How many cars, do you think?"

"Only saw two."

"Better odds. Let's move."

Logs stays even with Paulie for a few hundred yards, then, without warning, it all comes crashing down, the cold and the earlier workout, his energy *swirls* out. With one last burst, he catches Paulie's foot.

"What?"

"I'm not gonna make it."

"Logs, there's no choice."

"I can't, Paulie. I'm done. It's shutting down."

"Oh, God."

"Don't do that. Listen . . ." His voice quivers. "I can make it back to the ski float. Keep swimming. Remember, if you see car lights at the fire, stay north. Firth and his friends won't know what they're talking about. Wait them out, then get someone to call 911 and get somebody out to me. If I can get out of the water I'll be okay."

"Man, the air is forty degrees. You'll fucking freeze to

death, if you can even find it."

"This is our *only* choice. If you don't get across this lake and get the word out about Rankin, a whole bunch of people are screwed. Now *do* it."

"I'll get somebody to you. You get on that float and hang on."

"I promise," Logs says, desperately hoping he can keep it. "Listen, remember how I always say we're a trial-and-error species?"

"Yeah."

"Well, not tonight."

Paulie watches Logs disappear into the night, then, powered by fear he strokes toward the far shore. He forgets Logs and Mary and poor goddamn Kylie and Hannah. His parents don't exist. *Just get your ass to that fire.*

Twenty strokes and look; twenty strokes and look; twenty strokes and look. The fire is directly in front of him each time. *Thirty* strokes and look, thirty-*five*.

Distance over water is hard to judge. Distance over water in the dark, nearly impossible. Paulie believes he's about a football field away from shore; maybe another twenty yards to the fire. But the fire dims.

A puff of white smoke.

Fuck. They're putting it out! They're leaving.

He strokes faster, stops. He treads, listens to the voices of kids as they head toward their cars.

He starts to yell, just as he sees two sets of headlights emerging from the trees, lighting up the dirt parking lot. He cuts immediately right—north—almost sprinting, amazed at what strength comes from terror. They won't hear him as long as their engines are running and they're talking. He can make it.

Paulie barely feels the grass against his skin as he crawls onto the shore like a gator. He lies still, listening. Friendly voices; some laughter. He thinks he hears his name.

Fucking hurry! he thinks. *I've got five minutes, maybe ten before my body goes into fucking seizure.*

He lies still, willing the numbness to remain, brings himself to his knees as a car engine revs. The two cars that just arrived turn slowly, sweeping the shore with their headlights. Paulie hugs the ground, then watches them move slowly back up the road.

He stands and runs, stumbling, falling, and scrambling back up.

"Firth!" It's a whispered yell.

Nothing.

He stumbles toward the lot. The numbness is subsiding.

"Firth!" Louder.

A car door slams, a flashlight sweeps the area, finds him.

"Bomb?"

"I need your help, man."

"Sweet Jesus, what are you doing? You here to get baptized? We do it with our clothes on. You know Arney was just here looking for you? Lemme see if I can catch him."

One of those cars was Arney. "No!"

"He was with some—"

"No," Paulie says. "Get me in your car and turn up the heat. I'm about to have a freeze-out. Some really bad shit has gone down that you're not gonna believe. You got your cell?"

"Yeah, but there's no service over here."

"Then haul ass. Mr. Logs is out in the lake and if we don't get someone to him in a *hurry*, he's gonna die. You drive and I'll explain. What did that fucking Arney say?"

The makeshift lot is empty now except for Ron's car. Paulie tiptoes across the gravel in his bare feet and opens the shotgun door, only to see the seat occupied by Carrie Morales. She says, "I'll get in back."

"Stay where you are," Paulie says. "You guys got a blanket in here?"

"On the floor on the right side," Carrie says, pointing to the backseat. "But it's covered with dirt and needles."

"I don't care if it's covered in dog shit," Paulie says. He begins shaking uncontrollably, can barely work his fingers enough to get the blanket around him. Teeth chattering, he says, "Tell me what Arney said."

"Just that it was real important to find you," Firth says. "He's been looking all over."

"Who was with him?"

"I don't know. There were two cars, a passenger in his and I don't know how many in the other. None of them got out."

"You're lucky," Paulie chatters.

"I thought it was a bunch of your buddies. Anyway, he said he needed to hurry back to town, but to give him a call if you showed." Firth hesitates. "Why in the world would he think you'd show? I've been trying to get you to YFC for four years."

"Arney speaks with a forked tongue," Paulie says. "He's into some sinister shit. Listen, Ron, I'm asking you to do a very un-Christian thing."

"Which is?"

"Lie your ass off."

"I remember how to do that. Who do I lie to?"

"If we run into Stack on the road, you haven't seen me and I'm not on the floor of your car under this blanket, okay? No matter what story he gives you. And man, we gotta hurry 'cause Logs is in serious trouble. Hand me your cell; the minute we're in range, I gotta get 911."

"It kicks in at the far end of the lake," Ron says, and, feeling Paulie's urgency, floorboards the accelerator.

Hannah turns toward home. She's been driving aimlessly, trying Paulie's cell and Logs's home phone again and again. She doesn't know what else to do. She just wants to see Paulie and wishes she had never spent a minute with Arney Stack. It was stupid revenge; the kind that would never work with Paulie anyway. God, she *really* wants to talk to him.

Running it over and over in her head, she doesn't notice the black Audi parked across the street from her house as she punches the remote that raises the garage door.

.17

Logs is disoriented. He sees the lights by Paulie's car in the distance, but can't remember where the ski float is in relation to them. He knew where he was on the way over. He kept the YFC kids' fire square in front of him. They weren't looking for the float; Paulie simply ran into it. Now he doesn't know if it's ahead or behind. He stops, treading, struggling to visualize it from shore. He's skied off it a thousand times; knows it's north of the landing. He looks back—the YFC fire is gone. He thinks of Gehrig, curled on the couch. He hasn't fed him tonight. If he doesn't get back, who will . . .

Can't think that. You're the only adult with even a hint of what's going on. He stops treading and slides into drown-proofing. Front float, face in the water, push down gently while raising the head, take a breath, front float again. Over and over. He could do this forever if it weren't so goddamn cold. *Where in* hell *is that float?*

Suddenly he lays back in the water and *roars*; a loud, long, guttural purge. None of those assholes can swim, and if they had a boat they'd be all over the lake with it. The searchlight sweeps and Logs follows it, looking for that black rectangular absence of light. It looms huge, barely six yards from where he hangs suspended in the water.

"This is 911. What is your emergency?"

"My name is Paul Baum," Paulie says into Ron Firth's phone. "I'm a student at Heller High School. I was swimming with one of my teachers at Diamond Lake tonight and he started getting hypothermia. We made it to that little ski dock anchored in the middle and I left him there to go for help. He's out there now, and he could be freezing to death."

"Is this a joke?"

"Ma'am, believe me, it's no joke."

"It's nearly eleven, young man. You're asking me to believe your *teacher* went swimming with you in the pitch-dark and he's still out there?"

"Some people were chasing us."

"What people?"

"Bad guys," Paulie says. He flinches at how this must sound. "And a cop."

"I can trace this number, you know. It's not funny to tie up this line. Hang up and I'll forget this little prank."

Paulie hears a click.

"Shit!

Carrie stares at him over the seat.

"Sorry. *Fuck*! Logs is going to die out there!" He bangs his head against the back of the seat, still shaking uncontrollably.

"Chenier's got his ski boat," Ron says. "It's always hitched to their pickup. We can get Logs ourselves."

"Go!" Paulie says. He calls his father, hears it ring until it goes to voice messaging. "Dad! Paulie. I know you don't recognize this number but call it back. Big trouble. *Big*."

"What can your dad do?"

"He can get that 911 lady to wake the fuck up," Paulie says.

"Shouldn't we just go to the police station?"

"I'm scared to do that. If Rankin is part of whatever this is, who else? We get the wrong guy and . . . these guys were serious, Ron. We took Mary's text to Rankin and the next thing we knew he was running us off the road."

"What do you think Stack has to do with it?"

"Shit you and I can't even imagine." Paulie is sitting on the seat now, pulling the blanket tighter to stop his teeth from chattering.

Ron's phone vibrates in Paulie's hand.

"Dad?"

"What's up? What kind of trouble?"

"Mr. Logs is out on the ski float in the middle of Diamond Lake. He's probably got hypothermia. I called 911 and they thought it was a prank."

"I'll call. What in the hell was he doing in the lake at this time of night?"

"We were being chased."

"What do you mean 'chased'?"

"Bad guys, Dad. Really bad. Way too crazy to explain, just believe me. They're up at the boat landing now. And one of them is a cop."

"He a city cop?"

"Yeah. Last name is Rankin. He's why they were after us."

"It's county jurisdiction at the landing anyway," his father says. "I'll alert them and the state troopers. You better know what you're talking about, Paulie. If this turns out to be nothing, there'll be hell to pay."

"It won't be nothing. The more people you can get up there, the better chance we'll have of getting Justin's boat in the water."

"Justin's boat?"

"It's the fastest way to get to Logs. He can't have much time. Just get as many people up there as you can."

"On it." The line goes dead.

"This is totally out of control," Rankin says into his cell. "We can't get to the teacher and the kid. They got into the lake somehow and I'll be goddamned if we could find them. Hopefully they froze to death, but we can't count on it. Stack says they both swim like fish." He listens. "They're the only ones who saw the Wells kid's text, along with Hannah what's-her-name. All bets are off. We gotta move."

He listens for several seconds.

"I'm outta here tonight. Woody's got the Wells kid, but that won't last. If he had the sack to kill her he would have already, so you can bet she'll surface. A whole bunch of prominent names in this town are going to get mentioned, and when she breaks, others will, too. I'm sure very few of these assholes—I mean customers—used their names, but some of 'em are real recognizable. They'll be offered all kinds of deals to get to us. You better disappear too; when this gets out they'll be after us with torches and clubs."

Beat.

"We knew this was the risk. I had my getaway planned a week after we got into this shit."

Another beat.

"Stack is on his own. The stuff with the Wells kid and the Clinton kid and those two classy girls from over at Highland were his brainchild. He knew what he was getting into. Hell, he gave us the classy bitches. Knew they wouldn't talk 'cause of the kinds of daddies they got; and he knew the best threats. That boy is one sick fuck."

Beat.

"I know. He didn't just want a piece of the action. He had a whole list of kids at school he wanted to take down. Gets off on screwin' his friends at the same time they're thankin' him. Smart boy."

Beat.

"Naw, he's no more loyal to us than them. They catch him, he'll squeal like a pig. He might be smart, but he's a goddamn kid. We gotta shed him. I'll call him to meet and pay him off. He's taking care of that Hannah girl. No point to it now but he left before we knew there was no chance to get to the teach." Rankin laughs. "Pleasure doin' business with you, too." He flips off the cell.

The light in Hannah's bedroom goes out and the door on the passenger's side of the Audi opens silently. A dark figure, familiar with the surroundings, walks silently across the street and around the house, looking for an entry point.

Logs lies curled in the fetal position on the rough wooden float, shaking, sliding in and out of consciousness, trying to solve the unsolvable. The water temperature is warmer than the air; it has to be. But water is dense and therefore exudes greater influence on body temperature. Any mammal's inner heater has a better chance against air than water. Or is it the other way around? Air. Water. Density. Gehrig. How warm that little fuzz ball would be to lie against right now. All those women. The ones he should apologize to. He always meant to. It was selfishness; the reason he's dying alone. He needs to tell the kids. The Period 8 kids need to know what to avoid. Paulie and Hannah; especially Hannah. Zero tolerance of anything is, well, zero. He needs to warn the Wellses. Kylie. *In danger. Ah, Mary. Where are you, Mary?*

He sees himself as a young man, always believing he

had one more chance, and then pretty soon, all his chances were spent. *Concentrate on the good things. You did some good things.* Consciousness comes and goes in soft waves. It's so goddamn cold, and then it's not.

Justin Chenier's stepfather, Landry Faulk, approaches Diamond Lake at twenty-five miles above the speed limit, Justin turned around in the seat beside him watching the ski boat bouncing like a toy as they shoot down the two-lane. Paulie pulls on a set of Justin's sweats.

"Don't know who we're gonna run into at that dock," Landry says, "but I'll swing around and back this baby in before anybody can say shit to me. If there's trouble—hell, if there's trouble or not—y'all jump in the boat. Paulie, you undo the safety chain and unhook the hitch; Justin, you crank 'er up and go."

"What if—"

"No what-ifs. If Mr. Logs is on that piece of wood, he's in a *bad* way. Blanket's in the boat; you get it on 'im. That man been nothing but good to us—to *you*—and he gets payback." He pats the U.S. Army forty-five in his lap. "Didn't think I'd ever have reason to use this again an' I hope I don't, but nobody's gonna fuck with y'all an' nobody's gonna fuck with Mr. Logs."

• • •

As they crest the hill directly above the loading dock, heads turn and men scramble, some moving toward their cars, others bracing themselves. Landry Faulk doesn't know what he's coming into but he's coming fast. He wheels the pickup toward the dock, swings the full one-hundred-eighty degrees to point the back of the boat directly at the water, hits reverse, and backs in. Men yell. Three jog toward him. With one eye on the side window and the other on his rearview mirror he backs the trailer into the water.

"Go!" he hollers, and Justin and Paulie pile out, Paulie running for the hitch and Justin for the wheel. In seconds the boat is floating and the engine roars to life.

Paulie is still pulling himself in when Justin hits the gas and turns in a tight circle for the ski float. Justin flips on the running lights, but with no headlight, there is nothing to show the way.

"Your stepdad gonna be okay?" Paulie hollers over the engine and wind.

"*Hell* yeah," Justin hollers back. "He'll tell 'em war stories. If they don't like those, he'll give *them* some to tell."

Paulie peers into the watery darkness. "A little to the right, I think. Slow down, we don't want to crash into it."

"Hard to see," Justin says, squinting, then, "There!" He guns the engine a little, then cuts it, coasting toward the small wooden platform.

On it lies a still form.

Hannah turns restlessly in her bed. She keeps her phone in her hand, speed-dialing Paulie's number every five or ten minutes, calls that go straight to voicemail. A tapping below her second-floor window causes her to get up, peer into the darkness. Nothing. Paulie used to come by late every once in a while and throw pebbles at her window. She would sneak out and they would park down the block. She'd give anything . . .

Kylie's in danger. How in the world would Mary Wells know that? *Who* in the hell *is* Mary Wells?

She hears a rustling outside again, pads back to the window, and looks out wistfully. She knows it's nothing, either the wind or a cat. But she wishes. . . .

"What're y'all doing up here so late?" Landry Faulk stands facing seven men, none eager to test his willingness to use the forty-five dangling loosely in his hand, and none knowing how much he knows.

"We had an investment group meeting tonight," Rick

Praeger says. "We were meeting at the LDS church and we decided to have a drink." He smiles. "Obviously we couldn't have it there, and The Lantern was closed. So we just came up here."

"Be more than happy to have a drink with you," Landry says. "Who's pourin'?"

The men steal uneasy glances at one another.

"Lordy," Landry says, "somebody forgot to bring the booze?" He pushes his baseball cap back with the forty-five. "Which one of you is Rankin?"

The men once again glance uneasily at one another. Praeger says, "Who's Rankin?"

"The guy who brought you up here," Landry says. "One of you him?"

"He got called away."

Landry nods. "Those two boys are coming back in a minute with a man who might be pretty sick. That won't mess up your party, will it? Any a' y'all have a problem with me takin' 'em all out of here right quick?"

"I don't know what you think is going on," another man says, "but nothing illegal's taking place here."

"What I think doesn't matter," Landry says back. "I know three or four of ya, and I'd recognize all y'all in a lineup, which we all know would never happen 'cause nothin' illegal's goin' on."

"He's breathing!" Paulie yells. "Help me get him in the boat." He grabs Logs under the arms and drags him to the edge of the float. Justin stands in the boat with the open blanket while Paulie tips Logs in, then jumps in beside him, wraps him up tight, rubbing briskly. "Come on, Logs. Come *on!*" He yells to Justin, "Go!"

And Justin hits the throttle.

Landry hears the roar of the boat engine speeding toward him, looks to the top of the hill to see flashing red and blue lights, followed by sirens.

"Be damned," he says. "Look who's here. Any you guys feelin' like a 'person of interest'?"

Several men break for the trees and Landry laughs, turning to see the boat emerging out of the darkness.

"Dad! He's breathing, but he's out!"

"Paramedics comin' right atcha," Landry yells. "Stay in the boat with him!"

The EMTs back their vehicle toward the loading dock at Landry's direction, and in seconds two of them wheel a gurney toward the boat.

The men who didn't run stand wide-eyed in bright lights as state and county police take names and demand IDs. Three cops dash into the woods after the runners.

Paulie steps behind one of the EMT trucks, then slips away to the Beetle, reaches under the seat for his keys, starts the engine, and follows the wailing siren.

Nearly two hours later Paulie leaves the hospital hugely relieved. Logs will make it: he's unconscious, but his vitals are good. Paulie reaches for his iPhone, remembers he doesn't have it. *Oh God! Hannah would have called his number and Rankin would have answered.* Fuck! *I should have called her from Ron's phone.* He slams his fist into his palm. *Nobody even knows she's involved in this.* He races toward his car. *She's gotta be in trouble— on Rankin's radar if he answered my cell.* The screen display would have said simply "Murph." Rankin wouldn't know who that is . . . unless he's talking with Arney. . . .

I can't fucking think! Cops will be looking for Rankin but they won't know to cover Hannah. He starts the Beetle, speeds toward Hannah's house. *I'm gonna make sure she's okay and then I'm gonna find Stack. He's gotta be going to jail for whatever the fuck he's into, but before he does, I'm gonna kick his ass.*

.18

Habit forces him to park a block away from Hannah's house even though her parents are probably asleep. He can get to her by throwing rocks at the window.

He closes the car door gently, leaves the Beetle unlocked to avoid the short horn beep, and walks down the block. The living room light glows dimly through the pulled curtain and he tries to guess whether it's Hannah or her parents who are up this late.

Then he spots Arney's car parked directly across the street. He crouches, rushes into the bushes of a neighbor's yard, waits. Seeing no movement inside the car he steals up on the driver's side from behind. Empty. Arney is either lurking outside, or he's gotten in. The light in the living room this late makes the latter more likely. *Please, God! If you're there . . . Please!*

He slips back across the street and moves into the flower bed below the living room window, raises his head, hoping for a slight part in the curtains.

No such luck.

He circles to the back of the house. If Arney's in there, he had to *get* in, which means an unlocked window or back door somewhere. One by one he tests them.

A low window at the back of the house swings loosely on its hinges. Paulie props it open with a stick and drops into the unfinished basement, standing still as death.

He hears voices. Stealing up the stairs, carefully placing his weight at the outer edge of each step, he pictures the layout; this staircase opens into the kitchen, across the room is a swinging door leading to the living room.

He steps into the kitchen.

". . . shouldn't have done that." Arney's voice. "You made me hurt you."

He hears a man groan, a woman sob. The groan has to be Hannah's dad. The sobs are her mother's.

"Your daughter and I are going to take a ride," Arney says. "If you call the cops, or if the cops just happen to show, I'll kill her. You know I'll do it. Soon as I think I'm far enough gone, and if you folks haven't been stupid enough to send for help, I'll let her go. Understand?"

"Arney . . ." Hannah's voice is low.

"Shut the fuck up! You did this! If you hadn't been calling Baum like the two-timing bitch you are, I'd have just disappeared."

"I told you—"

"I said shut up. It's not you I'll hurt. But you'll watch." He nods toward Hannah's sobbing mother.

Hannah is quiet.

"Better," Arney says. "Now let's go."

"Oh, God, please! Arney, no!" pleads Hannah's mom.

Arney laughs. "Sorry, you just don't sound sincere."

Jesus! Paulie pushes the door open a crack, sees Mr. Murphy on the floor, a pool of blood under his leg, Mrs. Murphy kneeling beside him. A shadow fractured by light from the chandelier tells him Arney and Hannah are moving toward the front door. Like a cat he's back across the kitchen, down the stairs, and pulling himself up through the basement window. Arney has Hannah and Arney has a weapon, and Paulie can't think of a way to call for help without getting Hannah hurt. *This is off-the-charts crazy. Psycho crazy.*

He dashes across two backyards to get far enough up the street to cross undetected, then sprints through two more back lawns toward the Audi, emerging only yards away. He crouches next to a lilac bush and waits.

". . . better kill me, you son-of-a-bitch, because I'll find a way to get back at you."

Shut up Hannah! Just shut the fuck up!

Hannah's hands are bound behind her, but she's still Hannah. Arney presses the barrel of a pistol against her head and says, in the coldest tone Paulie can imagine, "Oh, I'm gonna kill you, baby, but slow. I'm dead anyway, so I'm gonna enjoy this. Fuckin' Period 8. I'd take out all you pussies if I had the time." He laughs again. "I don't have the time, but I have you."

"You were never going to let me go," she says.

"You think?"

Paulie hears her whimper then, "You asshole."

If they get in the car, she's done for.

Arney drags Hannah to the passenger side, opens the door, and pushes her into the backseat. Hannah kicks at the door. Arney's back is to him for a split second but Paulie freezes, almost as if he's anchored to the grass. *Jesus! MOVE!* Hannah kicks to get out, but falls backward onto her bound hands. Arney cracks her forehead with the butt of his pistol, slams the door, and rushes around to the driver's side.

Paulie springs at the car, screaming as he dives headlong over the low roof and into the side of Arney's head, spilling him onto his back. He grabs a handful of hair and slams Arney's head into the pavement, once, again, then drags him up by the shirt, throws a shoulder into his gut, and pounds him against the car. As air *whooshes* out of Arney, Paulie hears a distant, "Kill him, Paulie! Kill him."

Arney's laughter pierces the chaos as porches light up and men in pajamas and underwear rush into the street. "Kill me, Paulie! Kill me, big boy!"

Living room lights, then porch lights continue to flick on in neighboring houses as he pummels Arney, until someone yanks him back by the shoulders. He shakes him off and dives on Arney again. Two men join forces to pull him back. Arney struggles to rise while Hannah kicks her way out of the car, yelling as she hits the pavement, "The guy on the ground has a gun!" Arney scrambles for it, but someone kicks it away. "Paulie!" Hannah yells.

Paulie slumps on the street in the grasp of the two men. "He was going to kill her," he whispers, nodding toward Hannah.

One of the neighbors shoves a knee between Arney's shoulder blades, forcing him hard against the pavement, and calls 911.

"Hey, Bomb," Arney yells, spitting into the pavement. "Gotcha. Big stud! Cool jock dude! Fuckin' teacher's bitch! Guess who orchestrated your blissful night with the Virgin Mary. And guess who told your honey who you cheated with." He laughs again, blood running freely from his nose and from a cut on the side of his head. "Guess who made the Virgin Mary not a virgin in the first place." He spits blood. "Man, I had that bitch locked up. Guess who helped her figure out she was a whore."

Paulie's heart is in his throat. "Guess who's going to jail," he says weakly. "And guess who's going to be waiting if you ever fucking get out."

"Oh, I'll get out," Arney says. "And all the time I'm in there I'll be thinking of shit to do to you when I do."

"You are one sick fuck, Stack."

"Don't ever forget it."

.19

Paulie, Justin, and Hannah sit on the dock on a warm spring day less than a week after the national media circus has left town and things have begun to calm down; pants rolled up, legs in the cold water, trying to make sense of it.

"How does this happen under our noses?" Hannah asks. "I mean, you're right, Jus, anyone who says 'It can't happen here' is a clueless douchebag, but I keep thinking all this was going on while we were living our regular lives." She shakes her head. "Mary, Kylie. You gotta hate yourself for not getting to know them better. At least I do."

Justin shakes his head slowly. "It's amazing when everything you think turns out not to be the truth. Man, I've had a buzzer going off deep inside me about Arney long as I can remember. But I just thought it was because he was a shithead of the *normal* kind."

"I know," Paulie says. "When all this shit started coming out about him, there wasn't any part of it that didn't seem right."

Justin looks at Hannah. "Lucky, lucky lady," he says.

Hannah leans back, both hands on the dock propping her up. "You should have seen him at our house," she says, tears rimming her eyes. "My dad jumped up when he threatened me and Arney just shot him. He didn't hesitate. I feel so lucky it was only in the leg, but I don't think Arney would have hesitated to kill him." She shakes her head. "You should have seen him."

"Just remember he didn't," Paulie says. "Your dad's gonna be okay and everyone's alive. I wanna know who set the fire at Kylie's. That's the guy I want drawn and quartered."

"My bet's Stack," Justin says. "Or that fucking cop."

"Heard anything about her?" Paulie says to Hannah.

Hannah shakes her head. "God, I wonder how long she's been sitting in class wanting to tell somebody. And where is Mary? I sure could've been nicer to *her*."

"She's somewhere, I bet," Paulie says, "and I'll bet

we'll hear from her again. The news said all the bad guys fingered Woody as the 'brains' behind the sex ring stuff, but none of them thought he was a killer. Rankin, yeah, but not Woody."

"Profiler dude on CNN said the same thing," Justin says. He kicks the water. "I woulda bet ol' man Wells had a hand in it there for a while, but I guess I just didn't get him."

"He *did* have a hand in it," Hannah says. "Raise your kids so they can't think and sooner or later, your kids will be in trouble. At least that's what Logs says."

"Yeah," Paulie says, "we'll probably hear from her, but I'll bet she's never the same."

Justin nods. "All the happy endings are taken."

They look around at a junky turn-of-the-century Chevy cresting the hill. Paulie stands, waves. "Bobby Wright," he says. "Told him to meet me up here."

"Did he raise his hand and ask if you really meant it?" Hannah says.

"Gonna turn him into a channel swimmer," Paulie says. "Don't be dissin' my man Bobby. He's a work in progress. Been spending a little weight room time with him."

Justin laughs. "How's that workin'?"

"It's gonna take a little more time in the weight room," Paulie says.

The door to the Chevy opens and Bobby steps out. "I didn't know you guys were up here having a meeting," he says. "I could come back later."

"We're havin' a meeting, all right," Justin says, "but you're invited. Step right up here."

"Got your suit?" Paulie asks, looking down at the others. "A *lot* of work in progress."

Logs watches from the back of the room as Period 8 slowly fills up on the last day of regular classes.

When everyone's seated and into their lunches, Bobby Wright raises his hand.

"Bobby, I'm begging you, put your hand down. Spit it out."

"What are we gonna do?" Bobby says.

"About what?"

"Some of these guys are graduating, but the rest of us are still here. What're we gonna do with no Period 8?"

"Bravery doesn't just last a few days, Aquaman," Justin says. "That's what you'll do. Be brave."

"You don't need a classroom," Hannah says. "Mr. Logs

sleeps through half these things anyway. You can meet any time, any place you want."

"Yeah," Justin says. "Do it like the Thumpers." He points to Ron Firth. "Those guys'll meet in a *barn*." He laughs. "They do midnight campfires at Twisted Crick."

"And a damn good thing, too," Paulie says.

"Always happy," Firth says, "to light the way."

Hannah turns to Logs. "Do you think we'll ever hear from Mary? Do you think she's alive?"

"God, I wish I knew," Logs says. "Conventional wisdom says Woody Hansen took her. He's gotta be watching television, so he knows the law knows everything he's been into, the sex ring, the drugs, everything. Killing her could only make it worse." He pauses and thinks a moment. "If Rankin didn't find a way to hook up with them."

The room is silent.

"Mr. Wells is putting considerable resources into finding her. Money can make things happen. I'll pass along anything I learn." He shakes his head. "I just don't know."

"How did Arney fool us like that?" Marley asks. "I mean, we elected him student body president. And knowing he's been in Period 8 all this time, hearing us talk about our lives, makes me feel . . . I don't know . . . shitty."

Logs smiles, a smile devoid of humor. "I don't know if Rankin found Arney or Arney found Rankin. You can bet they recognized each other on first sight. Guys like them have radar for human weakness and they feed on it. Arney Stack is a guy who will tell you a brilliantly conceived lie and then have nothing but contempt for you for believing it. People are objects to Arney. He learned early how to *imitate* things like care and intimacy, but he never *felt* either of them. Arney Stack is among a very small and very dangerous percentage of humanity. He's twice as good at deceiving as anyone is at detecting him. And I'm with you all the way, Marley. I hate that he poisoned this place."

"Desert's a beautiful place at sunset," Justin says, "but rattlesnakes live there."

"My man," Logs says. "King of the metaphor. Truth is, there aren't a lot of people in the world like that, and you guys have already run into two of them. Statistically, you shouldn't run into many more." He shifts in his chair. "Look, if we let this drag us down, the bad guys win. That's a cliché for a reason. Time will help. Somebody finding Mary would do wonders, or seeing Kylie come out of the hospital with some strength." He gazes around the room.

"Look at the good news: Hannah's alive, and her dad will fully recover. Arney's going away, and I'm not frozen fish food. That's a start." He exhales. "We all know how vulnerable we are now. That's not necessarily a bad thing."

Tears well in Hannah's eyes. "What are we going to do without you? Whether we're staying or going, this is it."

"I'm retiring, not dying," Logs says. "I have the same telephone number in the same house with the overgrown lawn—in case any of you wants to bring your mower over to show your appreciation."

Marley says, "Mr. Logs, if you were going to give us all one piece of advice to take out of here, what would it be?"

"Advice about what?"

"Anything. One thing."

Logs thinks a minute. Then, "Don't listen to me."

Marley frowns. "What?"

"That's my advice," Logs says. "Don't listen to me. I'm an old guy. Turn me loose and I'll want you to learn from my experiences. I'll remember things that happened to me in my time and think I should warn you. But that's all BS. There is one teacher in this world and that teacher *is* experience. Mine for me, and yours for you. So that's it. Don't listen to me. Go out there and try stuff."

Marley smiles, looks at Hannah. They execute a synchronized eye roll.

"I gotta give you one more," Logs says.

"One more what?"

"Piece of advice."

"Okay."

Logs raises his eyebrows and points straight at her. "Stay alive. Do whatever you have to do to stay fucking alive."

There is a collective gasp. *No* one has heard Logs use that word in class. Paulie's heard it from him plenty of times out in the world, but never here.

Logs shrugs. "Last day. What can they do to me?"

The bell rings and students rise to leave. Logs stands at the door receiving high fives, fist bumps, and hugs.

"We in the water this afternoon?" Paulie asks as he passes.

"In over our heads," Logs says back.

Paulie pulls his car to the curb across the street from Hannah's house and watches as she secures her single scull to the top of her car.

"That ought to hold it," he hollers as she gives the last strap an extra tug.

Hannah shades the sunlight with her hand. "Hey, Paulie. I thought you guys were going to meet me at the lake."

Paulie gets out, starts toward her.

Hannah walks to meet him and they stand facing each other in the middle of the empty street.

"I made a promise to God that night," he says, and swallows hard.

"Yeah?"

"That if He'd help me save you, I'd be willing to give you up; quit wishing, *whining*, you know, aching for one more chance."

Hannah smiles, eyes watering. "*That* was dumb."

"But then I remembered . . ."

"What?"

"I don't believe in God."

Hannah puts her arms around his neck there in the middle of the street and holds tight. Paulie can't tell if she's laughing or crying, but he doesn't care. All he knows is, her arms are around his neck.

"I don't know how this is going to go," she says into his ear.

"I don't either," he says. "I just know it's got a lot better chance than it did a minute ago."

•••

Mary Wells wakes in a dark motel room, listens for the man's breathing.

Quiet.

She finds her cell on top of the dresser, grabs it, and walks outside into bright sunlight. She crosses the parking lot to the busy four-lane on the outskirts of . . . wherever she is.

She crosses the street to a Denny's, takes a booth, and orders coffee, discovers from the waitress that she's in Chico.

She takes out her wallet. A hundred twenty dollars and change, and her mother's Nordstrom's card. She sets the phone on the table, picks it up again, and dials her area code and the first three digits of her dad's cell, stares at the screen.

Several young people burst through the entrance, laughing and teasing. One of the girls wears a letter jacket from the local university.

She watches them fill a booth, snatching menus from each other, looking . . . free.

She looks out the window at the passing cars and feels a weight lift. The waitress brings her coffee. "You okay, sweetie?"

Mary smiles and nods, thanks her, and puts the cell back into her purse.